Thirteen Desperate Hours

A Liberty Ship's crew and their Navy Armed Guard fight for survival while grounded on a Japanese-held island

THIRTEEN DESPERATE HOURS

A Liberty Ship's crew and their Navy Armed Guard fight for survival while grounded on a Japanese-held island

by

Marill Johnson

Sunflower University Press®
1531 Yuma • P.O. Box 1009 • Manhattan, Kansas 66505-1009 USA

Printed in the United States of America on acid-free paper.

Cover: The Liberty Ship *John W. Brown* in convoy off the East Coast, April 1944, by John Stobart. Image courtesy of Maritime Heritage Prints, Boston, Massachusetts.

ISBN 0-89745-258-5

Sunflower University Press is a wholly-owned subsidiary
of the non-profit 501(c)3 Journal of the West, Inc.

My Sincere Thanks To . . .

The many Merchant Mariners and Navy Armed Guard members who encouraged and/or critiqued my story. A special thanks to . . .

- Captain Patrick A. Moloney, Master of the SS *Jeremiah O'Brien*, National Liberty Ship Memorial, San Francisco, California.
- Lyle E. Dupra, author of *We Delivered*, and his experiences as a Navy Armed Guard aboard a merchant ship.
- Captain Paul J. Esbensen, Master of the SS *John W. Brown*, and President of "Project Liberty Ship Inc.," Highlandtown Station, Baltimore, Maryland.
- Captain Arthur R. Moore, author of *A Careless Word . . . A Needless Sinking*, which describes so well the fate of other ships mentioned in my story, as well as 733 U.S. Merchant ships sunk during World War II.
- The Maritime Heritage Prints of Boston, Massachusetts, which allowed me to use their painting, "The Liberty Ship *John W. Brown* in Convoy off the East Coast, April, 1944," by John Stobart. Anyone who ever sailed a Liberty ship will get a cold shiver of pride just looking at this wonderful artwork.

. . . And a lifetime of thanks to all the unsung heroes of World War II, Merchant Mariners, and Navy Armed Guard, who gave their lives attempting to deliver their vital cargoes.

Foreword

AT THE CONCLUSION of World War II, historians wrote of the almost unbelievable successes of the United States Merchant Marine ships, which had delivered their cargoes through seemingly impenetrable enemy blockades. These ships were responsible for the Herculean task of transporting the bulk of supplies necessary to maintain our troops and allies in their effort to fight the war around the world.

The men that manned the ships included the Armed Guard, a specially trained branch of the U.S. Navy, which numbered about 24 men per ship, and the civilian volunteers, about 40 per ship, who made up the deck, engine room, and steward's departments. Civilian mariners could be any age, with any manner of physical impediments, or 4F classified as unenlistable in any of the U.S. military

services. As long as the men could do the job they had signed-on for, they were accepted into the Merchant Marine.

During the war, General Dwight D. Eisenhower honored the contributions of the Merchant Mariners and their Navy Armed Guard with these words:

> Every man in the Allied Command is quick to express his admiration for the loyalty, courage, and fortitude of the officers and men of the Merchant Marine. When final victory is ours, there is no organization that will share its credit more deservedly than the Merchant Marine.

General Douglas MacArthur, Fleet Admiral Ernest J. King, and many others, gave similar praise for the hazardous duties performed by these Mariners and their Armed Guard.

Yet despite their courage in the midst of harrowing, sometimes hopeless circumstances, almost no *action* stories are found that describe any of the 733 U.S. Merchant ships sunk by enemy fire.

Of the 2,710 slow, plodding Liberty ships built during the war, 174 were sunk by enemy action. An additional 72 were hit by Japanese Kamikaze planes, torpedoed, or otherwise battle damaged, but were able to stay afloat and deliver their cargoes — as was the ship in this story, the *Albert A. Robinson.*

All of our other military services are deservedly represented with exciting narratives, but no tales have condensed the often hair-raising events to show the men of the Merchant Marine and the Armed Guard as they joined together in their battles for survival.

This is a story that had to be told, a part of World War II about an unheralded service that suffered casualties in 1942 through 1943 proportionally greater than in all other branches of our Armed Forces combined, with the exception of the U.S. Marine Corps. These men of the Merchant Marine and U.S. Navy Armed Guard were heroes who must be remembered too.

After the death of my mother in 1996, I came across the letters I had sent her during the war. Reading them brought back many memories. In the South Pacific at age 17 doing T-2 Oil Tanker duty was where my letters started. As a Merchant Marine Radio Operator with heavy responsibility, my adventure began.

It wasn't until my third ship that one of the letters I wrote inspired my co-author (my wife) to make it into a book.

I had made two eight-month trips on the Liberty ship SS *Albert A. Robinson*, under Captain Robert Daly, the best of the best when it came to Captains. The other members of the crew, though their names are changed for my story, sailed with me on either my first or second voyage on the *Robinson*. Some of their eccentricities were so memorable, they were such colorful characters, that I did my best to visually describe them in print. Cramming them all into *Thirteen Desperate Hours* became a challenging project of recollections brought to light while reading my old letters.

The *Albert A. Robinson* never was hit by a Kamikaze during its actual error of straying 100 degrees off course. However, 17 Liberty ships, and numerous other types, had been hit in the prior three months of the Philippines campaign. This, coupled with the stories told me by those who had survived these attacks and had witnessed the heroic accomplishments of their crews, encouraged me to use some of that material in my story. And thus I have embellished portions of war's reality with the melodramatics of what *might have happened* in the various departments during the time frame of *Thirteen Desperate Hours*, had the *Albert A. Robinson* been hit by a Kamikaze.

This story is fiction . . . founded on a lot of fact.

Chapter 1

JANUARY 8TH, 1945 — The first American troops have landed on the island of Luzon in the Philippines. That night a small convoy of eight ships, led by two destroyer escorts, made their way through the Mindanao Straits between two Japanese-held islands, carrying vital supplies to the invasion point.

Placed at the rear of one column because of its volatile cargo of munitions, the Liberty ship SS *Albert A. Robinson* battled against the massive waves and whipping winds of a vicious tropical storm. Moving through the night at a controlled nine knots in the usual wartime blacked-out condition, the ships could not see each other through the sheets of pelting rain.

Second Mate, Josh Silva, five-foot-eight and built like a linebacker, lurched down the companionway, his steps adjusting to

the pitch and roll of the ship. A seasoned seaman about 30 years old, he finally reached his destination, the wheel-house — the bridge. Stepping inside, Silva prepared to start the 0400 to 0800 morning watch.

The man he came to relieve was 22-year-old Ivan Brown, the Third Mate, a slightly built "towhead" fresh out of the Maritime Academy in California, and making his first trip as an officer.

As Josh entered the room, Ivan asked, "Josh, is that you?"

"Yeah." He squinted in the darkness trying to bring the Third Mate's outline into focus.

Ivan looked at the luminous dial of his wristwatch. "You're early. I hope you brought some coffee. I drank the thermos dry."

"I did. I thought I'd get here early, to look over that map the Convoy Commander gave us. We have to make an extreme course change when you come back on duty at 0800. I want to review it."

Ivan yawned. "Because the Mate and I jockeyed our schedules to cover your bout of diarrhea, I only get three and a half hours sleep before I have to be back on duty." He yawned again, then chuckled. "I'm sure I'll think of a good way for you to pay me back for the lost sleep."

Josh grinned. "I owe you guys big time. I've never had a case of the 'Johnny-green-apple-quick-step' like this one. No way could I have stood my watch. I'll bet in the last ten hours I've spent six of them sitting on the crapper, but I think the Kaopectate Doc gave me has finally put a cork in it."

Ivan blew his nose. "A couple of the seamen also came down with it. Somebody thought maybe the canned catsup had gone bad."

"Hmmph. Could be. I tried to kill the taste of the Australian bully beef and powdered eggs with the catsup." He shook his head. "I won't do that again!"

A short laugh escaped Ivan's lips.

Josh set his coffee on the shelf behind the wheel man, and asked how it went with him.

"Fine, Sir," Rork answered, then turned back to Ivan. "I guess the watch worked out OK for you. Since we're traveling in convoy, you didn't have to handle the navigational chores and shoot the stars."

Ivan stretched and yawned again. "With or without the convoy, there would've been no star-sightings. There've been no stars visible over the last twelve hours. Man, just staring out those black bridge windows trying to see something through the pounding rain has wiped me out. I need a touch of that coffee if I'm going to make it down to my bunk."

Josh retrieved the thermos from the shelf as Ivan pushed away from the window. "Let's go in the chart room. Your relief should be here any minute. And you can get your coffee below, Rork."

"I'll do that, Sir."

Josh followed Ivan into the chart room, securely closing the door behind them. Before switching on the lights, he partially closed his eyes, then opened them slowly, allowing them to adjust. Unscrewing the top to his thermos, he poured a swallow or two into it for himself, replaced the stopper and handed the container to Ivan. "Did I ever tell you about my first trip in a large convoy heading for Murmansk?"

Ivan shook his head as he took the thermos. "No, but the visibility couldn't have been any worse than it is tonight. You can't see a damn thing out there."

"You're right. I've never seen it this black before." He paused, thinking back to that previous voyage. "Anyway, we were making a course change at the end of my watch. I told the wheel man to roll her over thirty degrees to starboard at exactly 0400. About ten minutes later, out of nowhere, *SLAM! BANG!* Some Dutch freighter zigged instead of zagged and tore off our starboard lifeboats. We'd swung them out in readiness, in case we needed them fast." He ran his fingers through his hair. "Believe me, when you were on the Murmansk run you wanted to have all the life boats available."

Ivan rubbed the corners of his eyes. "Lucky for us we make no course changes tonight. You can't even see the bow!" Pulling the stopper from the thermos, he half-filled his dirty cup with steaming coffee. After resealing it, he wedged the thermos between two books on a shelf protected by a half-front of wood. He turned toward Josh. "What's this course change you were talking about?"

Josh, bent over the huge table that took up the entire far wall, thumbed through the charts stacked there. "Ah . . . here it is, the map the Convoy Commander marked up. It's going to be a hoot to see how the destroyer escorts maneuver this convoy into a one-hundred degree change in course. Fortunately, it doesn't take place until 0800 when it's light. But if this weather doesn't let up, visibility is still going to be a big problem. We have to go from 255 to 355 and that —"

Ivan, who'd just taken a mouthful of coffee, nearly choked on it. "To 355?" he shouted. "We're already steering 355 . . . I think." He hurriedly doused the lights and yanked open the chart room door. "Rork, what are you steering?"

"Just what you ordered when I came on watch, Sir . . . 355."

The two mates stared wide-eyed at each other for a moment before Josh stepped to the wheel to confirm the luminous magnetic compass reading. "Oh, crap." He whirled around to face Ivan. "Who told you to steer at 355 degrees?"

"The Mate, when I relieved him at midnight. I asked him what he was steering, . . . he said 355. When I went to the bridge I told Rork," he pointed to the wheel man. "I had no idea it meant a course change. I assumed we were already on that course."

"Well, you're eight hours ahead of yourself." Josh paced across the room. "Lucky we're at the rear of a column or we could have hit another ship. Let's get back in the chart room and figure out where the convoy is by now."

Josh stopped. "Maybe even more important . . . where the hell we are in these uncharted waters among these Jap-held islands?"

Sparks, the Chief Radio Officer, trudged the 20 feet from his room to the radio shack, prepared to stand his watch. When he entered he found Junior, his assistant, busily typing his final entry in the radio log.

"Hey, Junior, anything exciting happen in the last four hours?"

Junior was making his first voyage, and wasn't enjoying the irregular hours required to fill the 24 in a day by a two-man team. With no licensed Third Radio Operators available at sailing time from San Francisco, they were short-handed.

Junior looked up and grumbled. "I probably couldn't have heard anything if it did happen." He removed the earphones from his head. "That storm we're in has so damn many close lightning strikes, the static bursts coming through the earphones have almost made me deaf."

Another strike flashed just as Junior laid the earphones on the typewriter table. A burst crackled in the room. Sparks shuddered. He wasn't looking forward to putting those earphones on for the next four hours. He cocked his head when he heard loud voices coming from the nearby wheel-house. "What do you suppose the Mates are yelling about? It sounds as if they're about to come to blows."

Junior put his hands flat on the desk and pushed himself into an upright position. "Don't know. They started all that shouting just before you came in." He stepped away from the desk. "They better be careful or they're going to wake the Old Man."

Sparks stretched, reaching for the ceiling, then stepped aside for Junior to pass in the cramped quarters of the radio shack. "Another two days and we'll be off this lousy twenty-four hour, four-on, four-off duty. What I wouldn't give to get eight straight hours of sleep." He dropped into the chair Junior had vacated and slipped a new log sheet into the typewriter. Almost by rote, his fingers hammered out: *SS Albert A. Robinson, Call KVIZ 4 AM Jan. 8th, 1945.*

"I'm going to hit the sack." Junior called out. "I'll be up to relieve you at 0800."

Just as he turned to leave, the thundering sound of something hitting the ship reverberated and echoed throughout the steel ship.

The huge vessel shook and shuddered, tossing Junior into Sparks's lap. In less than five seconds the *Albert A. Robinson* ground to a complete stop.

"Oh my God. I think we took a torpedo!" Junior scrambled to his feet and headed out of the shack, then stopped in the doorway as Sparks spoke out. "I don't think it was a torpedo or a mine, — I think we ran aground! We're not pitching anymore."

Sparks was only 18, and already on both his third ship and third trip to the South Pacific.

Frantic yelling exploded from the bridge and chart room. The lights flickered.

Junior grabbed his slippers from the floor and quickly put them on. "I'll go see what's what."

"What the hell was that?" yelled Ivan as each man lurched forward at the sudden stop. Both headed for the outside starboard bridge wing to get a better look. Rain pelted them in sheets, typical of a tropical storm, so heavy they couldn't see the bow of the ship, let alone what they might have hit. They struggled up to the flying bridge, fighting against the rain and battering wind.

Josh yelled at the Armed Guard lookout standing on the outer wing. He normally would have been stationed in the forward gun tub, but the waves crashing over it had made that location impossible. "Did you see what we hit?" Josh asked him.

The man, dressed in full rain gear, thrust his arms to the side and shrugged his shoulders. "I haven't seen anything beyond the bow since I came on watch at midnight."

Josh saw an A.B. — an able-bodied seaman — coming across from the port-side wing. "Olson! Get up forward and see what we hit! When you get there call me from the bow phone." He pointed downward. "I'll be on the bridge."

Captain Robert Daly, a ruddy-faced man of about 30, on his first voyage as Master of a ship, stormed into the bridge, barefoot and still in his skivvies. Seeing no Mates around, he yelled at the helmsman. "What the hell happened?"

Rork, with both hands still gripping the large wheel, shook his head. "Don't know, Sir . . . the Mates are top-side to see if they can tell."

Rork's feeble voice barely carried over the noise of the storm that drifted through the open door. No sooner were the words out of his mouth than Ivan returned to the bridge, dripping a trail of water and squishing with every step. He'd been thoroughly drenched on his trip to the flying bridge.

Ivan froze when he saw the Old Man. "The rain is coming down so thick and heavy we can't even see if we hit another ship, Sir. Because we're not rolling, Josh and I are guessing we've gone aground on some uncharted reef."

Captain Daly reached the engine room telegraph in three strides. Grabbing the large brass handle, he swung it back and forth several times. The bells in the engine room rang out simultaneously with those on the bridge. He settled on the position, "Full Astern." Taking three steps back, he fumbled in the dark for the ship's telephone. Then quickly feeling for the switch that would connect him to the engine room, he vigorously turned the small crank on the bell activator. He paced as he waited for an answer. "What the hell is wrong with those jerks? Come on! Answer the damn phone!"

When the Captain got no reply, he tried to make a connection with another station . . . any of the ten other stations . . . to see if the phone system still worked. "Damn it! *Damn* it! I'm not getting a reply from anybody, anywhere. The friggin' phone system must be dead!"

Two feet from the phone was the old emergency brass voice tube. Daly put his lips to it and blew hard. The whistle sounded in the engine room, six stories below. "OK, OK, I know you guys heard that one . . . now answer it!" He drummed his fingers on the wall as he waited.

Gallagher, the Third Engineer responded to the call. "Hey, bridge, what happened? Some pipes broke, and we're filling up with steam down here. Did we hit something?"

"We don't know yet," the Captain yelled down the pipe, "but we need *Full Astern* right now. Didn't you guys get my signal on the engine room telegraph?"

"Sure we did, Captain. We're switching it over right now. It's not as fast as throwing your old Ford in reverse, you know."

Captain Daly heard the impatience in Gallagher's voice. Removing his ear from the speaking tube, he put his mouth to it. "OK, OK. I can feel the screw turning now. Why didn't you answer when I rang on the telephone? I hate these tubes."

"Because it didn't ring," a somewhat confused voice replied. "I was standing right next to it when the tube whistled. With all the damage we have down here, I wouldn't be surprised if the phone system has gone dead, too. I'll try calling you. If I get no answer, we'll know our only communication will be through the talking tubes."

"As you say," Captain Daly grumbled. "If it doesn't ring I won't bother to call you back." He took a deep breath before continuing. "Anyway, keep her going *Full Astern*." He released his thumb from the whistle and made his way back to the rain-shrouded windows. He could feel the big screw shaking the ship, but no reverse movement. How could he get the ship moving again?

He heard Josh slosh his way into the wheel-house, and barked, "What can you tell me, Mister?"

"Nothing, Sir. It's blacker than black out there."

"OK, let's get a man up to the bow. Where's the A.B. lookout?"

"He was topside. I already sent him forward to see what we hit." Josh whipped the water from his head and face.

The Captain nodded. "Good, but I think I'd feel better if you got up there too. I want to know exactly what we ran into." His crisp voice spit out the orders. "Call me here on the bridge from the bow phone. I need to know if it's working. The engine room phone is dead. If you don't get an answer, get back here ASAP. We've got to know what we're dealing with."

"I gotcha, Captain." Josh disappeared into the darkened companionway, lit only by luminous markers, and made his way through the midship housing to the main deck below. Bending against the wind, the rain running down his face like a cold shower, he struggled forward to the bow. There he found Seaman Olson looking over the rail. "Can you see anything?" They both searched the water below, trying to see what might have caused the ship to stop.

The big steam engine had the propeller spinning in full reverse. The ship shook from stem to stern as the screw churned the water in an effort to free her. The *Albert A. Robinson* shuddered and groaned, but she didn't move.

There she lay, stuck on something — surrounded by Japanese-controlled islands. Captain Daly jerked his hand through his short hair. He strained to see through the blackness of the stormy night, but the sheets of water running down the glass obscured everything. His heart raced, beating so hard in his chest he could feel it. He slapped his hands against the thick window in frustration. How in the hell could this have happened?

Chapter 2

THE VOICE TUBE whistled sharply. Captain Daly, still at the window, whipped around. Ivan rushed to answer the call. He pushed aside the whistle button and yelled into the mouthpiece. "Yeah. This is the bridge. What d'you want?"

The craggy voice coming from below belonged to the Chief Engineer. "Yeesus *Christ*, vot the hell is happening?" His strong Swedish accent made Ivan grin, in spite of the situation. "Let me talk to da Cap'n." His words were interspersed with the smoker's hack that plagued him.

Captain Daly strode over, grabbed the tube, pushed aside the whistle mechanism, and hollered, "Go ahead, Chief." He put his ear to the mouthpiece to listen.

"Cap'n, this whole damn place is alive vith steam! Ve have at least

seventeen ruptured lines. A crack's developing on the vater feed line to number 2! Ve can't keep the engine going more than a minute or two or ve'll destroy the number 2 boiler! I got to shut her down and make repairs!"

Recognizing the urgency in the Chief's voice, Captain Daly took only seconds to make a decision. "Since the ship hasn't moved an inch one way or the other, go ahead, shut her down; but keep up steam. We'll want to give it another try when the tide is high."

"Uh-uh. Can't do it, Cap'n. To seal up these broken water lines ve have to shut down number 1 and 2 boilers completely. Yeesus *Christ*! The whole engine room's a steam bath!"

"Hang on a second, Chief." He turned to Ivan. "I need to know when the next high tide is. Look it up for me."

"Yes, Sir." Ivan hurried to the chart room. About 45 seconds later he called out, "In nine hours, from 1230 to 1330."

The Captain hollered again into the tube. "Chief, you can shut down and make your repairs, but I have to have full steam in nine hours."

"Vot kind of miracle vorker you think I am? Yeesus *Christ*, it'll take at least three hours to cool dis friggin' monster so ve can vork on it. I don't know how many hours it'll take to repair the damage . . . one hour, five hours, even ten hours. Then five to six hours to get up steam again. You got to give us more time."

Captain Daly shut his eyes, mentally scanning the problem. He could see no solution. "Can't do it, Chief." In a firm voice he added, "Nine hours is next high tide. We gotta get afloat before the Japs spot us. I don't know how you can do it, but you're going to have to!"

No reply came from the engine room, but the Captain heard the loud clank as the Chief slammed his hand against the communications tube. One corner of his mouth curled up. He knew he'd given the Chief a near impossible task, but if anyone could do the job, that wild old Swede could.

A tap on the shoulder startled him. He whirled around, almost knocking down Junior, the Assistant Radio Operator, who had slipped into the darkened room unnoticed. "What are you doing here?"

The rookie operator took a step back. "What do you think happened, Sir?"

Seeing the fear in the young man's eyes, the Captain softened his voice. "We don't know yet. Go back to the radio shack and find out if any of the other ships in the convoy hit this reef . . . or whatever it is." He patted Junior on the back while nudging him towards the door.

"I just came off watch, Sir. I would have heard if they'd broken radio silence. I'll let you know right away if we hear anything." Junior had barely reached the doorway when he brushed past Curtis Cash, the First Mate, usually referred to as "the Mate."

Cash, a large, muscular man with a booming voice, weighed well in excess of 200 pounds and stood over six feet tall.

Ivan, caught sight of him and promptly confronted him. "When I relieved you at midnight, what course did you tell me to steer?"

Cash frowned. "255. Why?"

Ivan, his fists clenched at his sides, shouted, "You said 355! Ask the wheel man!"

"You're full of bullshit, you little fart. I said *255!*" He glared down at Ivan.

With pleading eyes and his hands held in a cradled position, Ivan turned to the helmsman. "You heard him, Rork. Tell him what he said when I came on watch."

Rork, barely 19, was worried. He didn't want to get in the middle of this. He looked first at the Mate, then at Ivan. "Sir, you were both in the chart room when I relieved Smitty. You came out and said we're steering 355, so I cranked her over to 355. I didn't hear what the Mate told you."

Captain Daly, in shock, stood dumbfounded as he listened to the quarrel developing between his First and Third Mates. He couldn't believe what he was hearing. He erupted. "My *God*, what are you saying?" he bellowed. "What's this crap about 255 and 355? You mean to tell me we've been sailing four hours at one hundred degrees off course . . . through uncharted waters, and skirting the edges of these Japanese-held islands?"

Ivan cleared his throat. "Well, you see Sir, when I came on watch the Mate told me —"

"You lying little sack of crap," interrupted Cash. "I told —"

Captain Daly slammed the heel of his fist against the bulkhead wall. "Shut up! Damn it! Both of you, just shut the hell up!" He looked from one to the other. Anger flashed from his eyes. "We can determine later which one of you is in trouble. Right now we have a bigger problem." He drew in a ragged breath through clenched teeth. "But it's for sure, one of you screw-knuckles is going to lose his friggin' license over this FUBAR!" It was literally Fouled Up Beyond All Repair!

As Josh staggered into the room, breathing hard from from his quick trip to the bow, the Captain immediately turned his attention to him. "What'd you find, Josh?"

Josh struggled to get his wind back. "Sir, it's . . .not . . . a reef," he panted. He inhaled deeply, two more gulps of air, before he could continue. "We're on an island!" Leaning over, with both hands on his knees to help him catch his breath, he continued. "Both Olson and I could hear the surf hit the shore and, when a lightning strike flashed, we could barely make out what looks like coconut palms a hundred to two hundred yards out."

The Captain shook his head. "Oh shit! I was afraid of that."

"I tried to ring the bridge from the forward phone. Since you didn't hear it, I guess we've got some broken wires or a short circuit somewhere."

"Yes, but we have a more pressing predicament that's just come to light." Captain Daly swept Ivan aside with his forearm. "Into the chart room, all of you." He stomped through the door and the rest meekly followed. "Close the door and give me some light. Get the chart the Convoy Commander gave us."

While the Mate pushed aside some papers, Ivan retrieved the chart he and Josh had recently reviewed and spread it out on the table. All eyes stared at the Captain as he studied the heavy black line outlining the convoy's speed, course, and exact times when the course should be changed and by how many degrees.

Not a sound escaped from any of the men.

The Old Man looked up. "OK, you two dimwits changed course at midnight, right?"

"There!" Ivan put his finger on the map. "See Captain, the Mate thought we were to change course at the beginning of my watch, which normally is 0800. I filled in for Josh because of his bout of diarrhea. That made the beginning of my watch at midnight instead. That must have been what caused the mix-up."

Cash grabbed the Third Mate's right shoulder and spun him around. Waving his massive fist two inches from Ivan's nose he shouted, "You little SOB . . . you say that one more time and I'll shove every one of your teeth down your throat!"

Ivan's Adam's apple traveled up and down his throat several times, his eyes wide.

Captain Daly banged his hand on the chart room table. In a low, steely voice that made it clear he'd not stand for any more argument, he told the men to stop. "I mean it! The two of you, knock it off! We've got a more serious problem to contend with than your finger-pointing pissin' contest about who's responsible for this mess we're in!" The intensity of his narrowed gaze silenced them.

"I don't want to hear another word from you two while I refresh my memory on how we were to arrive at our destination." He talked out loud as he ran his index finger from the starting point of the convoy. "We were to sail through Surigao Strait, past Mindanao to open waters in the Sulu Sea. Once far enough off the Jap-held islands, we were to head north along the west coast of Negros, Panay, Mindero, and on to Luzon and the invasion point at Lingayen Gulf."

He looked up for a second, then back to the map. "Here's where we were at midnight." He put his finger on the map indicating the spot. "We should have just passed Mindanao and were leaving the Surigao Straits. We were supposed to travel eight hours out into open water before turning north. We made the one-hundred degree turn north at midnight, eight hours early." His finger moved slowly along the course they'd steered.

"Let's see now . . . four hours puts us . . ." Chewing on his lower lip, he checked his calculation to make sure he'd made no mistake. "Oh, hell! We're beached on Negros."

He raised his head, his nostrils flaring as he took a deep breath. "The Japs hold this island and, as I recall, they have an airfield here. Only a reconnaissance field, I think, but an airfield none the less."

Stunned, the three Mates stared back at him in disbelief.

The Captain's lips thinned to a tight line where his mouth should be. He sucked in another deep breath. "Well, boys, let me tell you, we're in real deep crap if we can't get this tub off the rocks before the Japs spot us!"

Lieutenant Wagner, the tall, athletic ranking officer of the Navy Armed Guard, knocked lightly on the chart room door, then slipped inside. To avoid any excess light from escaping, he closed the door quickly, blinking as his eyes adjusted to the brightness in the room. "What happened, Captain?"

Captain Daly, his arms folded across his chest, wagged his head back and forth. He leaned back against the table with the map spread open on its surface and explained the predicament that faced them. "One of these boneheads," he pointed at the First and Third Mates, "made an error, and we've been steering the wrong course for the last four hours. It seems we've run aground, most likely on the Japanese-held island of Negros."

Wagner's face paled as he blinked his eyes in shock.

The Old Man pushed away from the table. "I see you recognize the seriousness of our situation. To make matters worse," he raised his half-closed fist, his forefinger extended, "when we ran the engines at full astern, we couldn't dislodge her. And as if that's not trouble enough," he lifted a second finger, "the wrenching quick stop caused serious damage in the engine room. The main boilers had to be shut down so they can make repairs. The Chief doesn't know how many hours it will be before we can make another attempt to free the ship." He lowered his hand and leaned back against the table. "It's going to be more than a few. If the repairs can be made quickly . . . and that's a big *if* . . . our best chance to try again will be in nine hours with the high tide."

Stunned, Wagner took a step back. He felt as if someone had sucker-punched him in the solar plexus. His stomach knotted as the full impact of their position sunk in. Need it be said that being beached on a Japanese stronghold did not bode well for the ship and her crew? Sweat droplets formed on his almost bald head. He rubbed his moist palms together. He swallowed once or twice before he tried to speak. "Captain, shouldn't we take to the lifeboats and head for open water? Our number five hold is loaded with munitions! If we take just one hit there, everything for a mile around us will be flattened, and . . ." he looked around the room, catching the eye of each man. "the ship . . . our crew . . . vaporized!"

A flash of fear skirted across the Captain's eyes before he brought it under control. He shook his head slowly from side to side. "No way, Wagner. Not on your life . . or mine!" His voice, almost a whisper, was forced out through a dry mouth and clenched teeth. "What kind of chance would we have? If we didn't get capsized by these high seas, we'd end up being targets for the Japs. Once they spotted the *Albert A.* and saw there were no lifeboats aboard, they'd come looking for us. They'd know we couldn't have gotten far in this weather."

He dragged in a hurried breath. "Besides, only one of the four lifeboats has a motor. Even that would have trouble making any distance against this storm. How far do you think a boat propelled by oars would get?" He wagged a finger at Wagner. "If they find us, they'll strafe us. You know damn well they will. After they've sunk a ship, their subs make a habit of ramming and machine-gunning the lifeboats." He clenched his fists at his side. "Remember what that ex-mate of the SS *John A. Johnson* told us at the convoy meeting?"

The Captain turned towards his deck officers. "You've no doubt heard the rumors of some of the atrocities the Japs are known to commit. We met one of the Mates from the *Johnson*. The sub that torpedoed them surfaced and rammed the lifeboats, then sprayed the survivors with machine-gun fire. He was one of the amazingly lucky ones who didn't get hit."

Wagner watched the Captain flex his fingers open and closed, then cross his arms and lean back against the table. The intensity of his gaze made Wagner squirm. They had always worked well together, but this decision by the Captain seemed suicidal to him. He took a deep breath. "I still say the lifeboats are our best bet for survival."

"There's no way they would allow us to live to sail and fight against them another time." Captain Daly pointed at Wagner. "You know that's right. I think it's better, at least for the time being, to stick with the ship. At least here, we have something to fight back with."

Wagner felt a little nauseous. The fist wrapped around his stomach squeezed harder. He scowled. "Stick with the ship?" He frowned. "If we're going to do that, couldn't we radio for air support? Though whether we'd get it or not is another question." He chewed the corner of his lip. "We've got to do something. We can't just sit here waiting for the inevitable."

Captain Daly sucked in a deep breath, squinting his eyes in thought. "Break radio silence?" He hesitated, shaking his head. "If we did that, you can be sure they'd pinpoint our location with direction finders. They'd be on us the second the storm lets up." He rubbed the backs of his fingers over his jutted-out jaw. "Nope, that's not a gamble I'm willing to take without instructions from Pacific Command." Captain Daly's lips formed a firm line as he continued to examine his options.

Wagner, knowing the Captain so well, could read each one; should he abandon ship and the needed cargo stored in her holds, or should he prepare to put up a fight in the hope that, with high tide coming, they could stall long enough to get themselves off the rocks?

Seconds went by without a word being spoken.

The Captain looked directly at Lieutenant Wagner. "I understand, but there are reasons, important ones, why we can't leave the ship. At least not yet, not until we've exhausted all possible ways to free ourselves."

Wagner lifted a questioning brow. "What could be that damn important?"

Daly extended his hand, palm up. "You were at the meeting when we were told how essential the pierced metal landing strip plates (PSP) we're carrying are to the invasion forces. They'll need those plates, *now stacked in number three hold*, to make a landing strip as soon as the Army establishes the beachhead. And I bet that will be sometime today or tomorrow." He paused, closing his eyes in thought. A moment later he straightened, his chin up, his eyes clear. "No, we'll not abandon ship until we're ordered to by the Pacific Command."

A combination of frustration and anger swept through Wagner. He pulled himself up to his full height, chest out and chin up in an overstated military bearing, and took a step toward the Captain. "Then we're going to have to prepare for one helluva fight," he barked. He paused long enough to drag in a deep breath, as did the others in the room. "Let me tell you what's going to happen as soon as this storm blows over if we stay here . . . *Sir*!"

He surveyed the room, making sure he had everyone's attention to hear his defense. Lowering his voice to almost a whisper, he held up the index finger of his right hand. "First, I'm sure the Japs have daily reconnaissance planes covering the area, searching for convoys or any military activity. When one of those 'Washing Machine Charlies' spots us, it's all over. Ground troops will be here within hours . . . not days . . . but hours. I'm sure, because we're a stationary target. They'll have bombers over our heads within three hours from the time the weather clears."

He pulled a handkerchief from his pants and wiped the sweat from his forehead. As he stuffed it back into his pocket, he fastened his gaze on the Captain. "You recall what the Convoy Commander said about what happened to the *John Burke* and *Lewis L. Dyche*?"

The Captain nodded.

Once again, Wagner spoke to the Mates. "Each of those Liberty ships was carrying munitions, just like we are. Two weeks ago, at Mindoro, each took a Kamikaze hit. The *Dyche* blew up with such force it sank nearby ships. I think his exact words concerning the *Burke* were, 'It disintegrated! Vaporized!'"

Making eye contact with each of the men enclosed in the room, he spread his hands, palms up, as if to say, "Don't you see?" His tone changed, almost pleading. "Suppose we do wait and then get the ship free. If the Japs have already spotted us, without any convoy or some Navy fire power, what are the odds of making it to Lingayen Gulf by ourselves? We're bound to encounter some of those crazy Kamikaze son's of bitches, and they'd blow us out of the water."

He stepped back and leaned against the bulkhead wall. Satisfied he'd presented a strong enough case to convince the Captain they should abandon ship immediately, he smugly waited for the order.

The Mates, mouths open, realizing the seriousness of their situation, looked from the Captain to the Armed Guard officer and back again, as they waited to see what the decision would be.

Captain Daly stroked his chin. Deep concentration showed in his eyes. He took a deep breath, the air escaping in a ragged sigh. "All of what you say sounds right to me, Wagner; but we're staying at least until high tide. We need to have another try at freeing ourselves." Again, he rubbed the back of his neck, then folded his arms across his chest. "Besides, your point about what happened to the *Burke* and *Dyche* really points out the need our fly-boys have for the bombs and assorted munitions carried in number five hold." He shrugged his shoulders in an apologetic motion, and looked at his deck officers. "We've got to give at least one more first-class try to get free . . . in nine hours, at high tide."

Wagner, stunned by the Captain's words, slumped against the wall. Nine hours . . . they had to wait nine hours before the Captain would even consider abandoning ship. He couldn't hold his anger in. He took two steps toward Daly. "Nine hours!" he snorted. "The window of opportunity to escape will be long gone before nine hours is up. You can kiss your sweet ass goodbye if that's your final word . . . *Sir*!"

Unfolding his arms, Captain Daly leaned forward, putting his face inches from Wagner's. "That's my final word. Since you're the gunnery officer, I'll expect you to come up with a plan for our defense until the tide comes in. You got that, Mister?"

Wagner straightened and stepped back. "Yes . . . Sir," he stammered. There was no use arguing any further. The Captain's decision had been made. Now Wagner would do the job the Navy had failed to train him for; prepare a defense against ground forces for the beached ship.

The Captain appeared satisfied there would be no more argument and leaned back against the table.

Wagner's mind raced to come up with an idea to protect the ship and crew. "I haven't had time to think about a ground force defense, but — for starters — I'd like several members of the merchant crew to volunteer to learn how to load ammunition into the twenty millimeter antiaircraft (AA) guns. It's customary. You might have a couple on board that have had hands-on experience on previous ships." He paused briefly to get his thoughts in order. "There are eight gun tubs. I hope and pray I'm wrong, but the odds are that we, the Armed Guard, are going to have casualties. We'll need men who know how to unload and reload the magazines, in case any of my crew become unable to do their job." The picture of a wounded man sprawled in one of the tubs crossed his mind. A shudder ran up his spine. "We might need another two men, one each for the fore and aft three-inch fifties."

The Skipper nodded. "Cash, pass the word among the deck crew and the Stewards' department. We'll need at least ten volunteers to serve as backup loaders on the twenty millimeters and the two big guns. Make it clear to them they'll only be needed if we have casualties among the Navy gunners."

"Yes, Sir."

Turning his attention back to Wagner, the Captain almost smiled. "That's a beginning." He remained leaning against the chart room table. "Is there anything else that comes to mind?"

Chapter 3

LIEUTENANT WAGNER had a thought, but kept it to himself. Having no desire to get shot down again by a determined Captain Daly, he needed time to think it through, make sure it would work. "Well —"

Josh, the Second Mate, cleared his throat. "Sir, could I make a suggestion? I haven't had time to really think this out. It might not be a good idea, but . . ." He held his right forearm level in front of his chest. "If we were to put as much weight back aft as possible, it might tend to raise the bow." To demonstrate what he meant, he pressed down on his elbow with his left hand, making his right hand raise. "That might help us get off the rocks."

The Captain smiled. "That's a damn good idea, Josh."

Josh responded quickly. "That's not all of my idea, Sir."

"OK." With a dip of his head Captain Daly waved his right hand in Josh's direction. "Let's hear the rest."

Obviously nervous, Josh cleared his throat again. "My thought was, if we took the heavy metal airstrip plates on the 'tween deck from number three hold — and put them on top of the number five hold cover, and all around it . . ."

His voice trailed off for a second as he drew in a breath. His head tilted to one side. His eyes squinted and clouded over. It became apparent his idea continued to unfold in his head.

His eyes brightened. "We could link them together just like they do when they make the airstrip. If we stacked them layer upon layer, we could make number five practically bulletproof to almost anything but a direct hit from a two hundred pounder." He grinned. "As I said before, that would shift the weight to the stern, which might help raise the bow and give us a better chance to get off the rocks."

"Fantastic idea!" exclaimed Wagner, thankful someone had come up with a viable suggestion. Anything, any plan of action that would prevent strafing aircraft from hitting the explosive cargo in number five and vaporizing the ship and its crew, sounded good to him.

The other Mates and the Captain gathered around Josh, pounding him on the back. "Good thinking, man!" they chorused.

Lieutenant Wagner's mind went into a semi-daydream. His thoughts of a minute ago — the ones he'd kept to himself — flashed in his mind. Knowing the truth of Captain Daly's prediction that the Japs would strafe them in lifeboats, he'd almost suggested the crew swim ashore, take cover in the jungle. Would that make sense?

He decided his thinking had been colored by the fear of the number five hold taking a direct hit and blowing them all into shark bait. With Josh's idea, that didn't look like the sure thing it had before. With layer on layer of those landing field strips covering number five, and all the area around it, it'd take a big bomb to penetrate that kind of protection. Besides, when the Japs discovered an empty ship with the lifeboats still aboard they'd know the crew was on their island, and hunt them down. The men wouldn't be able to put up much of fight; the enemy with rifles . . . the crew with rocks.

Josh's idea was far superior, and the best chance they all had to survive. Plus, those Army boys fighting to take the beach at Lingayen were going to need the metal plates as soon as they secured their position. They were relying on the *Albert A.* to get them there.

He took a deep breath, thankful he hadn't blurted out his idea to the group. He slapped Josh on the back. "I like your plan, Josh. You can count on the Navy men to help."

Captain Daly nodded. "I agree. Your idea is brilliant. All we have to do is put it to work." He turned to the Mate. "How heavy and how large are those plates, Cash?"

The Mate's brows furrowed. He scratched his head. "I'd guess they're about ten to fourteen feet long and maybe twelve to fourteen inches wide. Since they're pretty thick metal, I'd say they weigh one hundred fifty to two hundred pounds each." His frown deepened, narrowing his eyes. "They come in bundles of eight. We'll have to bring them up with the winches and put them on the deck. We can cut the straps there so we can handle the plates one at a time. But they'll have to be hand-carried aft. No other way to get around the midship housing."

The men in the room relaxed. The hint of a smile crept onto some faces, others grinned widely. Eager to put this seemingly workable plan into action, Captain Daly pointed to the clipboard held in the beefy hands of the Mate. "Cash, what's in the lower half of number three hold? Anything else with some substantial weight that can be carried back aft?"

The Mate ran his finger down the first page of the manifest, shook his head, then flipped to the next page. Halfway down it he found the answer. "It's wood, Sir, building materials: two-by-fours, planking, that sort of thing. Not enough weight to make a difference. But those landing strip plates — we've got tons of them on the 'tween deck cargo area."

Daly clapped his hands together, encouraged at the prospect of a chance. His gaze traveled around the room, taking in everyone. "The question is, can we get those tons of plates moved before the high tide hits? We'll have to work fast."

Nods of agreement went around the room.

"OK, then," the Captain snapped his fingers and pointed at Cash with his right hand and Ivan with his left. "You two go below. Cash, you tell the men to break into teams of three, and there'll be no goldbricking. Break out work gloves for everyone. Steel can have some mighty sharp edges. We don't want any cut hands that might keep a man from doing his job. We'll need every available man to get this done. No one sleeps! Every crew member will turn to; I mean *everyone!*" He chewed the corner of his lower lip as he continued to formulate and organize the task before them. "It's important you let the crew know our situation — we've run aground on an enemy-held island. That ought to inspire them to hustle and cut down on the possible bitching."

He shook his head. "Did I say everyone? I meant all but the engine room gang. They have their hands full putting those broken pipes back together."

He turned his attention to the gunnery officer. "Wagner, explain to your men that during this crisis they'll have to follow Cash's orders, at least until it gets light. If the weather clears enough for enemy air patrols, we know your Navy crew will have to man their gun tubs." With a smile, he raised his eyebrows. "You agree to the use of your men that way?"

"Absolutely, Captain. I'll let them know what they have to do and why."

Daly grinned, happy to see his gunnery officer so whole-heartedly behind this new plan. Their working relationship had always been good. He'd hate to see that change. The Armed Guard were the protectors of the ship, and they were under Wagner's command. It eased his mind to know there'd be no more insistence they abandon ship, and no more argument.

He turned to face the Third Mate. "Ivan, you supervise the clamping together of the steel plates. I want them neatly laced together, fore and aft for the first layer, port to starboard on the second. Alternate each level. Understand?" He placed his left hand over his right, his fingers at right angles, to demonstrate what he meant.

Ivan grinned. "Yes, Sir." Obviously this responsibility the Captain had bestowed on him, even after the 100-degree error made on his watch, cheered the young officer.

Captain Daly looked at the ceiling. He wondered what else needed to be taken care of. "Josh, call the engine room. Ask the Chief if we can have steam on the number three winches. It shouldn't affect his repairs. He has to have steam somewhere, or we wouldn't have any lights.

Cash started toward the door. "While I'm below, I'll dispatch a crew to start removing the strong-backs, tarp, and hatch boards off number three. We'll need those winches to remove the hatch beams, though. I'll also get Boats — the Boatswain — to get a crew working on the booms so we can start unloading onto the deck as soon as we have steam." He twisted around and pointed a finger at the gunnery officer. "I'll have the names of the ten men who volunteer to help man the guns within the hour. Let me know when you want them."

"Just a minute, Cash." Captain Daly rubbed the back of his neck. The strain of working out the details for their daring attempt had tightened his muscles. "You know, we've got to remain semi-blacked out, except for down in the hold. You won't have any large cargo lights to help you and your boys with the booms. They can use hand-held flashlights, but none of the big lights. We have no idea how far away the Japanese barracks might be. The longer we can keep them in the dark about our presence here, the better our odds of getting off this damn island."

He dug his fingers into the knots in his neck, trying to knead them out. "Tell the guys to be careful. In this lousy weather the decks will be wet and slippery. Because of the darkness, they'll be working almost blind. Make them understand how important it is that we do everything we can to get off this island. If we don't, we're going to end up being target practice. That ought to inspire them to double their efforts on any project they're assigned to."

"Gotcha, Captain." Cash disappeared into the darkness of the midship housing, Ivan trailing behind.

Josh blew hard into the emergency speaking tube to rouse somebody in the engine room, six stories below. He put his ear to the mouthpiece and tapped his foot impatiently as he waited for an answer. Some 30 seconds later he got it.

"Yeesus *Christ*, vot now?" the old Swede Chief shouted, then coughed and hacked for a moment.

Josh waited for him to catch his breath before speaking. "Chief, we need steam on the number three hold winches. Can you give it to us?" He listened intently, hoping for an affirmative response.

"Yah — OK, OK, in twenty minutes. Ve'll need to wrap one split pipe before I can turn it on. Ve vere able to maintain some steam on one boiler to give you lights and fire protection. I vill switch it over to also give you steam for the vinches. The other boiler vill remain shut down."

"I hear you, Chief, and thanks. Give me a whistle up the tube when the Bosun can begin using it."

"Yah — vill do."

He turned away from the speaking tube to report the conversation to Captain Daly just as the Old Man jerked his head in Josh's direction and snapped his fingers. "Josh, I've just thought of a couple more things we can do to lessen the weight on the bow." He lifted his eyes to the overhead in thought and took several deep breaths. "Ohhhh, *shit*! Maybe not. I was thinking of dropping the anchors, but they might get hung up in the rocks. Then we'd never get free." He shook his head. "No, let's forget them for the moment. We'll just work with my first idea. I want you to call the Chief back. Ask him if the forepeak tank on the bow is filled with water. If it is, tell him to empty it. Also, tell him if the aftpeak water tanks are empty, to fill them with salt water." He raised and lowered his outstretched hands to visually show the hoped-for results.

"Damn good idea, Captain." Josh slapped his forehead. "Don't know why I didn't think of it."

Captain Daly, making light of the situation, pressed his index finger against his right temple. "Well, the Old Man isn't exactly a dinosaur, you know. Sometimes I'm capable of using the ol' melon for something other than a hat rack."

"Touché, Captain." Josh chuckled as he turned back to the communicator tube. "I'll check with the Chief right now."

The only man on board officially semi-trained as a medic, was 32-year-old Doc Johnson, the ship's Purser and the Captain's secretary. Almost two years older than Daly, he'd become a good friend of the Captain. He walked into the wheel-house, his ever-present cigarette dangling from the exact center of his mouth. "Is the scuttlebutt true, Captain? Did we go aground?"

"'Fraid so, Doc, on Negros . . . currently held by the Japanese."

"Anything I can do to help?" Doc's cigarette wiggled up and down as he spoke. Sometimes a person paid more attention to the butt in his lips than they did to the man.

"Yeah. Go down and tell the Steward there'll be no food served in any of the mess halls. Ask him to brew up a major batch of soup out of that Australian Bully Beef he's been serving us lately."

He ran his fingers through his slightly mussed short hair and shook his head. "I'm afraid no one will have a sit-down meal 'til we get off these rocks." He rolled his tense shoulders, letting a deep sigh seep out. "Food on the run is the order of the day. Make sure the Steward understands that."

"OK, Captain . . . anything else?"

Daly laid a hand on Doc's shoulder. "I'm afraid that's not all. You'll have to set up the officer's mess as a hospital."

Doc frowned. "Hospital? What do you mean, hospital?"

"You'll be in charge of the sick-bay. Your combination office and infirmary is way too small. The puny hospital room, with four beds crammed into that tiny space, isn't compatible with what we might need. It's quite possible we'll need more space . . . a lot more."

Doc paled. His cigarette waggled frantically as he spoke. "You make our situation sound pretty serious. Is there something else I should know?"

Daly scruffed the back of his hand over his unshaven chin. "I hope I'm wrong, Doc, but let's be as prepared as we can in case I'm not. If we don't get this ship off these rocks before the Japs discover us, we'll be in deep, deep trouble."

Fear flashed briefly in the Purser's eyes. He swallowed twice and took a deep breath, letting it escape in a hiss. Slowly he nodded in understanding. "I see what you mean. What else do you want me to do?"

"Get the Steward to issue you all the blankets, pillows, mattresses, and sheets he has stored. Take all your medical books and supplies down there now."

"What medical supplies? My medicine chest consists of aspirin, atabrine, Band-Aids, and Merthiolate for jock itch." Doc shook his head, his brows coming together in a frown. "Not much to found a hospital on." He shoved his hands in his pockets.

Captain Daly tapped Doc's chest with his index finger. "Whatever you have, Doc, it all goes into the officer's mess: gauze, splints, iodine, burn salves, everything." He stepped back, pursing his lips. Again he massaged his neck. The knots had become tighter by the minute. "Check back aft with the Armed Guard. They have a stash of stuff you might be able to use. Scrounge up everything you can find to equip your makeshift hospital." He took a deep breath, as if he couldn't get enough, and let it out slowly. "I have no idea what the next few hours are going to bring. It makes good sense to be prepared for anything. Go set up the officer's mess. It's going to be our hospital until we get off these rocks and into open water." He put a hand on his friend's shoulder. "I'm afraid, and so is Wagner, you're apt to be busy as hell before this is over."

Doc hesitated. "I hope my limited training will be adequate, Captain."

"It has to be. You don't have time to learn any more than you already know. Just do the best you can."

Doc drew his brows together in concentration.

The Captain could see something troubled him. "What is it?"

"There's something I'm trying to remember." His frown deepened. A few seconds later he snapped his fingers, his wrinkled forehead relaxing. "Now I've got it. Is it OK if I draft Elijah, the black, Second Cook, to help me? He's actually a trained medic."

"He is?" The Captain's eyes widened. The corners of his mouth lifted slightly. "Now there's a talent I'm happy as hell to hear is on board. I'm sure you can use his help."

"I know I can. I've had long conversations with him. He really knows his stuff. He used to drive an ambulance in Harlem. He's treated gunshot wounds, stabbings, even some burns."

"How did we happen to get him in the Maritime Service? I'd think the military would have snatched him up."

"Lucky for us, the military classified him 4F." Doc's dangling cigarette flapped wildly with every word. "He'll be a big help if things get bloody. My knowledge on that subject is almost nil. My training consisted primarily of dispensing atabrine for malaria and other simple preventive medications."

He took his cigarette out of his mouth and squashed it under his shoe, the room still too dark to find an ash tray. "Elijah's also a Holy Roller. He quotes scripture all the time, and has a calming influence on everyone. He'll be good to have around if we have any serious casualties."

"OK, but tell the Steward what you're doing. Let him know the orders came from me."

Doc put another cigarette in his mouth and hurriedly left the bridge. As he disappeared into the darkened midship housing, Captain Daly whispered, "Good luck." His friend would need every bit he could get if things turned ugly.

Not long after Doc's departure, Captain Daly heard the chug-chug of the steam-driven winches, and the sounds of the pull of the steel cables against the heavy booms as they were swung into position to unload the landing strip plates. Though the rain still washed down in torrents, he went out on the bridge wing to look down on the activity taking place. His ear caught the "sing" of the steel cable as it strained under its first load. The sound filled him with a guarded pleasure. Finally, the plan was in operation.

Men from the deck crew, the Armed Guard, and Steward's department stood in the rain awaiting the first load. With a crash, the steel bundle landed on the starboard side main deck. Having already been broken into groups of three, the first team moved forward. Cash, strap cutters in hand, snipped the formed sheets from their nested packing. The men shouted "lift" in unison, and the first plate rose into the air. They trotted down the starboard passageway of the ship with their heavy load.

Ivan's team waited for them, standing on the number five hatch cover. Eager hands took the plate and placed it in position. The three-man delivery team scooted back for a second load down the port side, avoiding any chance of slowing the delivery of the next plate through the narrow passageway.

The Captain nodded in approval. His officers had done a good job of organizing.

After cutting the straps on the second load of plates, Cash stood with the clippers still in his hand. He waved toward the stern. "Move 'em out cowboys!" he shouted.

The words were barely out of his mouth when a lightning strike hit about 100 yards off the port side. Cash squeezed his eyes shut. The light was blinding bright. A crack louder than a cannon's roar almost deafened him. For one moment he stood in the center of light, then it was gone. He couldn't see, his pupils as small as if he'd looked directly into the sun. Slowly they widened as his eyes adapted to the blackness of the night.

"Did anyone get hit with that mother?"

The men stood frozen in place, rooted to the spot by the power of nature's fury.

Cash slowly brought them back into focus. "That baby was so close I can taste it! Sort of metallic." He worked his tongue across his lips. "Can you guys taste it?"

Two of the men spat on the deck. One said, "It tastes like I got metal filings in my mouth."

The three-man team that had been about to pick up a steel plate took a step back, pointing at it. Fearfully, one of them asked, "Mate, what would have happened if we'd had that in our hands? Would we have been electrocuted?"

Cash saw how frightened his men were. He couldn't blame them. That last strike had scared him, too. His heart pounded in his chest. He sucked in a breath when another fork of lightning lit up the sky a little to starboard. He felt the rumble of the thunder in his bones. Those bolts are too damn close, he thought. He looked at the crew, apprehensively waiting for his answer to their question. What could he tell them?

Another flash, another roll of thunder. He managed to appear unfazed this time. In order to ease the men's fear he had to shake off his own. He took two calming breaths before speaking. In a confident tone he attempted to reassure them. "I don't think so. Usually the lightning will strike the highest point and run down to ground through the metal." He smiled. "But you guys don't need to worry. They say 'lightning never strikes in the same place twice.' It's already hit here, so let's get back to work."

The three-man team looked cautiously at each other, then lifted the top plate and sprinted down the starboard side as if they were in a race. They seemed anxious to get the load out of their hands as quickly as possible. Cash grinned to himself. Could it be they didn't really believe the "old wives tale"? He waved his right arm like a cop hurrying traffic along. "Come on, next team, move it! *Move* it!"

Chapter 4

AN HOUR LATER the lightning had moved on and the rain, which had been a deluge, eased up slightly. Morning light glowed faintly through the clouds.

Captain Daly paced restlessly back and forth across the bridge, occasionally glancing out the windows. Although the men would now be able to see what they were doing more easily, he wished the violent rains of the passing storm would return. That would keep Japanese air reconnaissance on the ground. He had no desire to find out what might happen if a Washing Machine Charlie spotted them.

He paused halfway across the room, letting his hands rest on the bulkhead, and lowered his head to rest against them. The situation weighed heavy on his mind. Had he done the right thing? Should he

have listened to Wagner and abandoned ship? If they couldn't get off the rocks, what chance did they have as a stationary target? Between strafing and bombing they were doomed, unless they could shoot the attacking planes out of the sky. What were the odds of a merchant ship doing that?

I made the only decision I could, he thought. It's my responsibility to get this cargo to its destination. I had no choice but to order us to stay with the ship. He scratched his head. Disturbing thoughts tumbled through his mind. What about the responsibility to the crew — and their families?

It's not too late, he thought. We could still leave the ship and get everyone ashore. After we got on the beach we could sink the lifeboats, and head for the hills. Hopefully, there'd be a band of Philippine guerrillas up there we could join. When the Japs spotted the ship, and saw there were no lifeboats on board, they'd probably spend days looking for us on the open water. That would be safer than taking to the lifeboats like Wagner suggested. The odds of survival might be better on land. He shook his head. He knew they weren't high. But would it give the men a better chance than sitting on an armed, stationary target, should the enemy find them before they could free the ship from the rocks?

He rubbed his temples, attempting to massage away the developing headache. Why was he even toying with the idea of leaving the ship? They stood just as good a chance of surviving by staying on the *Albert A.*

He took a deep breath, pushed away from the wall and straightened his spine. His thoughts turned positive. *I'm Master of this ship. I worked hard for this position of responsibility*. He rubbed his hand across his tired eyes. *I believe I've made the right decision. We'll get off these rocks at high tide.* He clenched his right fist and smacked it into his open left hand. "Damn it! We *will*!" he said under his breath.

Sparks, earphones clamped on his head, sat typing the 0600 BAMS — the Broadcast to Allied Merchant Ships — schedule on his log sheet. His fingers paused for a split-second when he heard KVIZ, his call letters. What directive would be coming their way? He looked at his assistant. "Junior, go tell Captain Daly a communiqué will be coming in soon. He'd better have Wagner get the code books ready."

Junior, who walked with a limp, the result of a birth defect, hurried off-kilter the few steps to the bridge to relay the message.

The Captain nodded. "Have Sparks bring it to me as soon as you have it."

"Yes, Sir."

Junior spun around and hurried again, back to the shack, in time to see Sparks change the frequency on his receiver. The radio operator hunched over the typewriter, his fingers poised. When he heard his call letters he typed the five-digit code group numbers that followed. He pulled the completed message from the typewriter and removed his earphones.

"Return the receiver to the emergency standby frequency, Junior, and stick close until I get back." He hustled out the door and strode the short distance to the chart room. Looking around, he handed the piece of paper to the Captain, already stationed next to the high table. "Where's Wagner? This thing is in code. You'll need him to decode it, Sir."

Captain Daly looked at the jumbled mess of gibberish, a collection of letters and numbers, and shook his head. "You and I can muddle through this." He pointed at the two large code books he'd already put on the table. "Wagner's tied up getting ammunition ready for the twenty millimeters. Get Junior to stand your watch while we see what this baby has to say."

Sparks took a few steps to the door and yelled, "Hey, Junior, hold down the fort. It looks like I'm going to be busy in here for awhile." Circling back, he took up a position next to the big table. "OK, what do you want me to do?"

The Captain shoved one of the books toward Sparks. "You handle the letters book. I'll take care of the numbers. What page does the book say I should start on?"

Thirty minutes later both men leaned back, rolling their shoulders to relieve the ache from hunching over the table intently decoding the missive.

> *U.S. Navy Destroyer Escort 104 reports you disappeared from convoy PZ77 night of January 8th. What is your position and ETA Lingayen Gulf? Your cargo is urgently needed. Respond immediately on 2716 KC (Kilocycles). NAOL (Pacific Naval Command)*

Captain Daly reread the message twice out loud. "Damn, how do I know when, or if, we're going to get off this rock pile?" He leaned his elbows on the table and cradled his head in his hands.

Sparks licked his lips. "Sir, could I make a suggestion?"

"Let's hear it."

"Since we have to answer their message anyway, why don't we request their help to get us out of here. If they need our cargo so badly, maybe they'd send a destroyer or something to pull us off the rocks. That way we'd have at least one escort to the Gulf."

Captain Daly reached over and rubbed the stubble, only a quarter-inch long, on Sparks's head. In a time of levity the Captain had retaliated for a less then perfect haircut the Radio Operator had given him by cutting the young man's hair that short. "Damn good idea, baldy. Copy this down."

Sparks patted his shorn head. "At least it's cool." Grabbing a piece of paper, he removed the pencil he'd tucked behind his ear, licked the lead point, and held it in readiness. "Shoot."

The Captain cleared his throat. "*Albert A. Robinson* aground on Negros Island, 8.83 degrees North, 122.52 degrees East. Send vessel capable of assisting us to pull free of rocks. Sign it, Captain Robert Daly, USMS."

Sparks held out the note for the Captain to check what he had written. "Right?"

"Right."

"Sir, I can't send it this way. I wouldn't dare break radio silence with this information. Even with the odd-ball 2716 KC special frequency they want us to respond on, Japs could be monitoring it. It gives our position. We'd have Nips all over us before I shut down the transmitter. It'll have to be coded."

Daly lightly punched him on the arm. "I know that." For the first time since the grinding halt of the ship had awakened him, he laughed. This naïve 18-year-old tickled him. "Guess what? You're going to help me encode it."

"Me, Sir?"

"You. Open the first code book to the letters ALHCZ and give me the page number to apply to the second book. If we work together we can code this message in no time."

Sparks yelled down the companionway, "Thirty minutes more, Junior, then you can rustle us up some new coffee."

"Better hurry, I'm fading fast." Junior's faint voice drifted back, making Sparks grin. His assistant operator always over-dramatized things.

Sparks turned his attention to the book in front of him, rapidly giving the Captain the information he needed to write the message in code.

With the job completed, he hesitated before leaving the chart room. "Sir, you realize breaking radio silence could give the enemy the opportunity to triangulate our position. It's doubtful they would have three or more stations monitoring the frequency we've been instructed to use . . . but it's possible.

The Captain shrugged. "Either way, we have to answer their message. We'll have to keep our fingers crossed that this early morning transmission catches the Japs still half asleep so they won't have time to zero in."

Sparks held up his free hand with fingers crossed. "OK. I'm out of here."

Returning to the radio shack, Sparks slapped his assistant on the back. "OK, Junior, go stretch your legs, or whatever it takes to keep you awake. Then, get me some good, strong coffee. I have a hunch this is going to be a long day."

Sparks sat down at the transmitter console. After pounding out the series of dots and dashes that made up the coded reply, he sat back and waited for further communication from Pacific Command, questions churning in his mind.

Would they send someone to help the ship, or would the *Albert A.* and her crew be considered expendable?

During this time, in the engine room, the Black Gang — a name held over from the days when they shoveled coal and ended their watch covered with soot from the fire box — was hard at work under the watchful eyes of the old Chief.

"Yeesus *Christ*, you panty vaist. So a little hot vater dripped on you. Get back up there," he pointed at the overhead pipes, "and put another layer of plumber's tape over that cloth asbestos wrapping. She's got to be able to take two hundred pounds pressure, and it sure as hell von't the vay you left it." The Chief lapsed into another one of his coughing spells.

The Oiler scrambled back up to do as he'd been told.

The Chief's hacking subsided. He caught his breath and summoned Bob Crosby, the First Engineer. "Ve don't have time to replace these split pipes. Ve'll have to patch vith tape and clamps to meet the deadline the Cap'n has demanded. Got any suggestions?"

Crosby shook his head. Steam seemed to be spurting out every place he looked. "I'll gather up anything I think we can use and get back as quickly as possible. Do you have a supply of plumber's tape right here?"

"Yah, but ve can always use more — and bring all the clamps you can find."

A short time later Crosby returned cradling a box in his arms containing all sorts of hardware — C clamps, riser clamps, split-pipe clamps, worm-driven hose clamps, bench vises, vise grips, U-bolts, cloth asbestos wrapping, and more plumber's tape.

"This is all I could find, Chief."

"Good — good. Let's get busy. You take half the gang and vork on that area." He indicated one side of the room. "I'll direct the repairs on this one."

Crosby moved off through the thick curtain of steam.

The engine room, though its thermometer read 120 degrees, resembled the movie version of a bad night in London. The moist fog hung so thick you couldn't see from one end to the other. The hiss of escaping hot vapor filled the six-story-high room. Breathing became labored.

Since they had shut down boiler number 1 — and partially boiler number 2 — not enough time had passed for cooling. The pipes remained hot enough to cook on. The Chief pulled on a pair of heavy, leather work gloves. Every man working on repairs wore a similar pair. He started toward a spewing pipe, but a large split over the boiler caught his attention. "Gallagher," he roared.

The Third Engineer raced to answer the Chief's call. "Yes, Sir."

"Can you rig a Bosun's chair so ve can get that big crack up there?"

Gallagher surveyed the problem, then nodded. "I think so. I'll have to get one out of the Bosun's locker."

"Vell, vot are you vaiting for?" He waved him away. "Go . . . go!"

Gallagher, with a broad grin, gave a three-fingered salute, Boy Scout style, and hurried to the ladder, one of the four he'd have to climb to get to the main deck. Once there, he dug through the Bosun's locker and gathered the chair, hoist, and rope he needed and scrambled back down to the steaming heat of the engine room.

Near 0900 hours, the rain slowed down to a steady drizzle. With the sun making bright veils of white around the dark gray clouds, it appeared the storm would soon be over. Frowning, Captain Daly stared out the bridge window. Once again he wished for a return of the tropical storm. Some heavy wind and rain could buy them some time.

Wagner strode into the room, breaking the Captain's train of thought. "Looks like it's going to clear, Captain. A few patches of blue have broken through the clouds. I'd like to take the Armed Guard men off the duty of hauling plates. They need to ready their guns. Confrontation with the enemy is inevitable, we just don't know when. They need to be prepared."

"Of course. Tell Cash to let them go."

Wagner whirled around and disappeared as quickly as he'd come. On deck the three-man teams continued to run the airstrip plates to the number five hatch. He hurried to find the Mate who supervised the operation. "With the weather clearing, I have to pull my men, Cash. They need to ready their guns. Will you send them to the Armed Guard mess? I'll give them orders there."

Cash frowned, but nodded his agreement.

The 25 men under Wagner's command gathered around him, standing shoulder to shoulder in the mess hall. He looked from one to the other. "As you can see, the weather's clearing. That means we could get a visit from the Japs most any time. Once they spot us, you can be damn sure we'll draw their fire." He swung his gaze over the serious-faced young men again.

"We've practiced almost daily how to prepare the guns for action. Now, it's the real McCoy. It's time to go out there and make sure your weapons are ready for combat."

"Yes, Sir." The answer came in unison.

Wagner felt a rush of pride as the men hurried to their designated spots. They'd been well trained. In his mind he could see exactly what they were doing. Each 20mm two-man team would strip the rain cover from their gun, making sure all the critical parts were cleaned and well oiled. That done, they would recover the barrel to be sure no rain would get in it from the occasional quick shower that would periodically douse the ship. Next, they'd make sure several 60-round magazines were readily available.

Once the preparations had been completed, the teams took to jabbering with each other over the fire-control phone system. Wagner smiled. He knew the good-natured kidding, bragging, and joking kept the men loose and alert, but was also aware that their eyes continually swept the skies, searching for any sign of an enemy plane. They'd also comb the beaches in case a Japanese patrol unit should happen upon them.

As the tension mounted, so did the degree of boasting between the gun tubs. Challenges were tossed out and wagers settled on. Who would be the first to bring down a plane? Wagner shook his head. Typical youth.

The job of neatly layering the landing strip plates on the number five hold had moved into high gear. The stack now measured over four feet high, adequate enough to stop any mortar or small bomb's direct hit.

Ivan, the Third Mate, worked alongside his men. "Come on, guys. Put some hustle in it. The higher we make it the safer we all are. The thicker the shield, the better our chances. If a big bomb were to penetrate to the munitions in this hold we'd all be blown to Kingdom come."

The men, all visibly exhausted, groaned in unison. They'd been on the run for hours, but then, he had been working hard, too. Their lives were at stake. Ivan knew they all needed to keep going at 100 percent effort.

"Hey, Ivan, why the overkill? Who're you trying to impress? That barrier we've run our tails off to build is already thick enough to stop the biggest bomb the Japs have," a member of a newly arrived threesome shouted. The man leaned against the rail. "I gotta sit down for awhile. My ass is really draggin'."

Ivan glared down at the grumbler from his position on top of the metal mats. "Sanburn, you bung-hole, you're flat out wrong! A hundred and eighty pounder, a bomb even the Zero's carry, would penetrate this feeble stack." He knew he could order the man back to work, but chose to reason with him instead. "You're not seeing the whole picture, for Christ-sake! Think about it! We not only add more protection for this hold the higher we go, we also put more weight back here. Didn't anyone explain to you that raising the bow will make it easier for the ship to get free of the rocks? In fact, when we get the steel mats too high to handle on the hatch cover, we're going to load the rest of the plates all the way back aft."

A chorus of moans arose.

"I know you're all tired. But we have to protect this munitions hold. We'll keep stacking these plates everywhere they'll fit until the 'tween-deck of number three hold is empty. Is that understood?"

Sanburn nodded. With a grunt he helped the other two men in his team push the latest plate they'd delivered up to the top of the pile. "Come on, guys. It doesn't look like we're going to get any rest."

Ivan shook his head at the retreating figures, then turned back to help his team of assemblers place the new plate in position and lock it in place.

"Hey, Ivan, got something for you and your gang." Hogan, the Chief Steward, yelled as he and a helper bustled toward the busy mate with a large, stainless-steel pot and a tray covered with coffee cups.

"What's up?" Ivan smiled down on the approaching pair.

"Cookie brewed up a batch of thick soup. He calls it Bully Beef Borscht, or BBB."

"Sorry, Hogan. I appreciate the gesture, but my guys can't stop to eat." He started to turn away, but the Steward's voice stopped him.

"They don't have to. That's what the cups are for. Let them fill one before they start back for their next load and drink it on the way. When they've downed it, they can put the cup in their pocket. When they need some more nourishment, they can get another scoop."

"That sounds like it might work."

"The Captain said this is all we'll get for today. There'll be no sit-down meals."

Ivan tipped two fingers to his temple in a good-natured salute. "I'll explain the process to each group as they deliver their load." He placed his hands at the small of his back and leaned backward to relieve the strain. "Is everyone going to have to come here to get their BBB?"

Hogan stepped back to make room for the team arriving with the next load of steel. "No! Only the cargo workers and the aft Armed Guard. We're taking pots up forward, to the flying bridge, and one down to the engine room."

"Sounds like you've got everything all figured out. Would you hand up five cups of that — what did you call it? — Bully Beef Borscht — for me and these guys?" He gestured with a sweep of his arm at his four assemblers.

Five cups were quickly filled and handed up to the men on the hatch.

"Thanks, Hogan. Will you explain the system for food on the run to these guys who just got here? I'll tell those that follow about it."

While Hogan ladled out cups for the newly arrived men, he told them the plan and what the cups held.

"Bully Beef! Can't we get something decent to eat?" one of the men grumbled. But he changed his manner after tasting it. He gulped the contents of his cup and took a little more before racing to catch up with his teammates who were already on their way back to get the next load.

At 0945 hours the men still hustled to move the steel plates, get them positioned, and get the number three hold emptied. Sounds of frantic work filled the air: the clank of steel on the decks, the yelling of the work crews, the chug of the winches, followed by the singing of the strained booms and cables.

Within seconds it abruptly came to a halt.

The drone of a single-engine plane could be heard in the distance. Silence prevailed as each man looked to the skies to locate the aircraft. "Is it one of ours, or one of theirs?" This question traveled from one man to the next.

Ivan pointed to a section of sky half-filled with clouds. "It's up there, off the starboard quarter, about one o'clock, passing just above the clouds." He shielded his eyes, trying to see more clearly. It passed through a patch of blue sky. "There! There it is! But I can't tell whose it is."

All eyes turned to where he pointed.

Chapter 5

LIEUTENANT WAGNER stood alongside the number four, 20mm gun tub, located on the forward corner of the flying bridge. He raised his binoculars and trained them on the elusive plane. "I can't identify it for sure. I only get quick glimpses between the cloud openings," he informed the two gunners in the tub next to him. "If I had to make a guess, I'd say it was Japanese. Fortunately, they didn't look our way. Probably kept their eyes scanning the sea, looking for subs, convoys, or Navy ships. We lucked out this time."

He followed the flight pattern of the plane until he could no longer see or hear it. Noting its direction from north to south, he lowered his field glasses. "I bet it just took off from the airfield on Negros."

Grimly, he turned. "We won't continue to be so lucky. Make sure those guns are ready."

"Yes, Sir." The two men once more checked the condition of the weapon they would man in case of an attack.

As the sound of the aircraft's motor died away, Wagner was glad to see all hands resumed their tasks. A sense of urgency now prevailed. He could feel it. No one moaned or complained, but everybody set about getting what needed to be done finished as fast as possible.

He descended the ladder from the flying bridge to the wheel-house where he found the man he wanted. Before Captain Daly could speak, Wagner said, "I can't be sure, but I'll bet it was Japanese. It was too far astern, and with the cloud cover, I couldn't get a clear look." He took a deep breath, letting it out slowly. "I'd say we dodged a bullet this time, pardon the pun. We won't be so lucky forever. Another Washing Machine Charlie will find us sooner or later."

"I was thinking much the same thing. One of them is bound to spot us if we don't get off these damn rocks soon."

"With that thought in mind, I'd better get together with the ten men who volunteered to back up my gunners so they can learn what they'll need to know. I'd like to put them in the gun tubs now. With the Navy teams already at their stations, the coaching will be easy and fast."

Captain Daly nodded. "Good idea."

"I'll only take three at a time, so it won't slow up the hauling too much. It shouldn't take more than ten minutes per man to teach them how to change the cartridge drums and assist on the big guns."

"Sounds sensible to me. The weather's clearing. There'll probably be more plane activity as soon as it does." The Captain looked up at the clearing sky through the bridge window.

"You know, I never thought I'd ever wish for a vicious storm, but right about now some heavy winds and rains would be mighty welcome." He turned away from the window. "Since it doesn't look like we're going to get them, we'd better get those volunteers into your gun tubs."

Wagner waited while Captain Daly swept his gaze over the deck below. "I saw Cash a few minutes ago, talking with Boats, but I don't see him now."

"Will you tell him what I want? He doesn't have to take orders from me, and wasn't happy about releasing my men from the cargo moving job. I'm sure he won't want to let anymore go."

"Hand me the speaking trumpet. I'll get his attention."

Wagner grabbed the trumpet from the corner and handed it to the Captain, who strode out onto the flying bridge and called, "Cash — Cash."

Down on the deck the Mate raised his hand to stop the winches. "What can I do for you, Cap'n?" he yelled.

The Captain shouted back, "The clearing weather is going to give us a problem. The men who volunteered to back up the gunners need to be given instructions. Send them to the Armed Guard mess hall, three at a time. They'll meet with Wagner there. Shouldn't take more than ten to fifteen minutes. Then you'll get them back."

Even from the bridge, Wagner could see the scowl on Cash's face as he acknowledged the order. "Thanks, Captain. I'll get your boys squared away and be back up here as soon as I can." He paused in the doorway. "Let's hope their backup won't be needed."

Captain Daly nodded. "We can only hope."

Junior walked in the door of the radio shack with a fresh thermos of coffee he'd gotten from the galley. Earphones clamped on his head, his fingers busily typing the 1000 hours BAMS schedule into the log, Sparks motioned for him to put it down and wait. "We've got a message coming in after this. I want you to copy it with me so we're sure there's no mistake in one of the hundreds of numbers transmitted."

"OK." Junior spread a piece of paper on the console table and balanced himself by leaning a hip against it. With a pencil poised in readiness, he waited.

The BAMS schedule ended. Sparks laid the earphones on the desk as he flipped the switch to put the Pacific Command transmission on the speaker. "It's not as clear this way, but we'll both be able to hear it now." Changing the frequency of the receiver as he'd been instructed, he rolled a fresh piece of paper into his typewriter. His fingers hovered over the keys as he listened for his call letters.

KVIZ de NAOL sounded from the speaker in a series of dots and dashes.

"OK, Junior, here it comes. Copy all of it."

Both men listened intently, writing or typing as rapidly as the dots and dashes filled the room.

Junior thrust his paper toward the Senior Radio Operator as the Naval transmission signed off.

"Keep it. I'll call off what I copied." Sparks pulled the paper from the mill. "See if it agrees with what you have."

Sparks read the first groups of letters and following series of numbers he had typed.

Junior diligently followed along on his own message. "Perfect. We both heard the same thing."

Sparks stood, stretching the muscles that had grown tight from sitting so long on his watch. "You'll have to hold down the fort for awhile, at least until I find out if the Captain needs me to help him decode this. Wagner may not be available."

"Will do."

He strode the ten steps it took to reach the bridge, and thrust the page with its myriad numbers out for Captain Daly to see. "Here's the response from Pacific Command. Do you need help in decoding it?"

"Yeah. Wagner's off on another project. He's tutoring the merchant crewmen who volunteered to load the twenty-millimeters and the three-inch fifty." He jerked his head in the direction of the chart room.

Sparks followed the Captain through the door. Pointing at the squat, round pot surrounded by several coffee cups resting in the center of the high table he asked, "What's that?"

The Captain's gaze turned to where Sparks pointed. "Oh, that. It's some Bully Beef soup. Try some. It's not bad." Grabbing one of the code books, he shoved the other in toward the radio operator.

Sparks shook his head. "Maybe later. Let's get this thing decoded." He reached for the paper the Captain had dropped on the table, and code book number one.

"I'm curious as all hell to find out what Pacific Command has to say. Maybe it's good news. We could sure use some."

He ran his finger down the string of five-letter codes until he found the right one. He gave the page in the second book they'd use to decipher the message. After a concentrated effort, the decoded message lay on the table.

All warships engaged in active duty. Have dispatched two LST's from Mindoro to assist in pulling you free. Their ETA, 1700

> *today. Proceed to Lingayen immediately. Cargo urgently needed. NAOL.*

"Son of a bitch!" Captain Daly slapped his hand on the table. "LSTs are just troop landing ships. They're capable of putting lots of troops ashore, and carrying all sorts of rolling stock, but can they help us? I don't know what kind of horsepower they can generate. I'd sure feel better, much better, if they'd sent a destroyer escort or two." He took a deep breath. "They'd have gotten here a lot faster, too."

Sparks shrugged. "You never know, Captain. Those LSTs look like they can move pretty fast when they have to. Their horsepower may surprise you."

"Maybe you're right." He looked sideways at Sparks. "It looks more and more like our effort at high tide better do the job. If it doesn't, we might be in big trouble. I don't see how we can sit on a Jap-held island until five tonight and not be detected. That's more luck than we can hope for." He spooned some soup into a cup. "Besides, I don't believe in luck. Luck is the hope of fools. We've simply got to free ourselves. We can't rely on luck, or those LSTs, to do the job."

Sparks paused in the act of filling a cup with soup. "You're right. There's a lot to be said for making your own luck." He took a sip of the thick, hot liquid. "Hey, this tastes pretty good. Is it OK if I take a cup back to Junior?"

The Old Man extended his hand, palm up. "Be my guest."

Troubles still plagued the engine room. The seemingly tireless old Chief stood on the grate floor below, urging his men, suspended from makeshift scaffolds, to perform the near impossible task of repairing the damage in record time. He chose to ride his best friend, the Second Engineer, knowing the man would understand. By picking on him, the others would sense the urgency, and understand the necessity for speed in making these repairs. "Yeesus *Christ*, can't you move any faster than that, Mr. Svenson? Ve don't have all day, you know!"

"You know, Chief," Svenson called from his perch alongside the big boiler, "you could do me a big favor."

"Yah, vat's that?"

"Throw me two or three of those potato sack rags so I can put them across my legs. The steam droplets coming out of this pipe are almost boiling. My legs are beginning to look like boiled lobsters."

The Chief grabbed four sacks, wadded them into a ball, and threw them up to his Second Engineer. He paused long enough to light a cigarette, then, between coughs, bellowed, "Now, vill you please finish that damn job. I have another vun I want you to vork on."

Svenson quickly wrapped his legs with the sacks. As he went back to work, he mumbled under his breath, "Stick it in your ear, you salty old reprobate. If this joint's going to hold, it's got to be done right. That takes time."

Several workers who were in earshot of the remark laughed. Even the old Chief heard enough of it to make him smile, as he started up the ladder leading to a big bank of batteries. Perhaps there lay the problem with the communications system, he thought. If so, he could try to repair it. Getting the phones back into working order would eliminate the need to use the speaking tube system. "It's a pain in the arss," he muttered to himself.

Just then the hollow "clank" of a one-foot monkey wrench landing on the steel grate not more than four feet in front of him jolted the Chief. His head jerked up to see where it had come from. "Ye viz! Vat are you trying to do, Mr. Crosby? Kill me?"

"Sorry, Chief," the First Engineer apologized. "The friggin' thing slipped out of my sweaty hand when I put the final torque on this damn nut. Just leave the stupid thing there. I'm finished with this split and I'm coming down. It's too damn hot up here, Chief. I'm actually feeling a bit light-headed. I gotta get some water." He struggled to his feet from his sitting position. "Look out below." He dropped the other tools he'd been working with onto the grated deck, then climbed down to the lower area.

"Vell, is that patch going to hold, Crosby?" The Chief squinted his eyes to study the completed work and evaluate it.

"You can bet your cantankerous Swedish butt on it, Chief. That baby's not going to give us anymore trouble." Arriving at the Chief's side, he paused. "After I get a long drink of water, I'm gonna get that one." He pointed to a hissing pipe off to his left. "And that's gonna be a bugger."

Captain Daly glanced at his watch. 1045.

"What the hell?" The loud voice seemed to come from the flying bridge. He scrambled up the ladder in time to hear, "Go away! Go back to your village."

Lieutenant Wagner, speaking trumpet in hand, spoke forcefully to a group on the beach. He turned as the Captain approached, and pulled the trumpet away from his mouth. "What the hell's wrong with those damn kids? They're coming right down to the water's edge."

Captain Daly reached his side and looked toward the beach. A group of youngsters he judged to be between 10 and 13 years old, had emerged from the jungle and marched in a straight line toward the ship. "What's going on, Wagner? What are those kids doing here?"

Wagner sighed. "I've been trying to get rid of them. Obviously, they're natives, curious to see who we . . . Oh hell! Here come four more." He pointed to an area off the starboard side. He took a deep breath and let it out with a whoosh. "I've got to get them to leave. If Japanese ground forces show up, some of those kids are going to get killed."

Captain Daly nodded in agreement. "I heard you tell them to leave. I wonder how we can get them to go home, or wherever they came from?"

Wagner raised the trumpet again. "Go back! It's too dangerous here. Go . . ." He gave up. "I don't know what to do. Those little farts aren't paying any attention to me."

A voice came out of the number four gun tub right next to where they stood. "Probably, because they can't understand English, Sir." The dark-haired man who'd been checking out the gun stood up and turned towards Wagner.

Wagner smiled. "You could be right, Martinez. Negros is a pretty remote island. What language do you think they speak?"

"In Northern Luzon they speak Tagalog, but here, in the Southern Philippines, a lot of people speak Spanish."

"Do you know of anybody on board who knows the language?"

Martinez grinned. "I'll give it a try. I speak Spanish. It won't take long to find out if they can understand me. If they don't, we can get Raul. He's from Manila. They should be able to understand one of us." He jumped out of the gun tub and took the speaking trumpet from Wagner. "But you know, the Spanish I learned is the language of Mexico."

Wagner nodded. "Go to it. Tell them to go home. This is not an invasion to free them from the Japanese. If they don't leave they could get injured, or even worse, killed." His eyebrows came together in a worried frown. "Impress on them they should not tell the Japs we're here. In fact, they shouldn't tell anyone."

"You want me to tell them all that?" Martinez looked from Wagner to the Captain and back again.

"Not really, but as much as it will take to get them out of here."

Martinez raised the bull horn to his mouth. The Spanish words flowed fluently from his lips to the children, who now stood at the water's edge. "Hey, you kids, if you can understand me wave your arms."

Fourteen arms fanned the air, the children eagerly jumping about and laughing.

Wagner couldn't help but smile at their exuberance. "They seem to like whatever you told them, but they're not leaving. See if you can do something about that."

The gunner's grin widened. "I wanted to find out if they could understand me . . . apparently they do. Now I'll try to get them to move." He raised the speaking trumpet again, speaking rapidly in the language they understood. "This is an order from General Douglas MacArthur! You must return to your homes immediately, and you must not come back! Do not tell anyone about our ship being here! That's an order from the General. Now, go home! Go right now!"

The youngsters turned on their heels and ran back to the wooded area from whence they had come, never even pausing to look back.

Martinez faced Wagner, a wide smile on his face. "My mom sure would be proud if she could see me now."

"What did you tell them?"

The gunner explained what he had said.

Lieutenant Wagner half-smiled. "Nice touch, Martinez." He took back the truumpet. "I'd forgotten how MacArthur is almost a god to these people." He faced the Captain. "Let's hope that's the last we see of any villagers."

"I'll second that!" Captain Daly started down the ladder to the bridge. "In fact, let's hope that's the last we see of anyone on that beach . . . period."

Wagner and Martinez agreed.

Captain Daly, alone in the wheel-house, paced back and forth. No helmsman stood at the wheel. It was hardly necessary, since the ship had run aground. They'd been conscripted, along with all other available hands, to move the steel plates back aft.

He looked again at his watch. 1100 hours. The time to make another try at getting free would be here before long. Would it be successful? If it wasn't, what should he do? The urgency of the situation sent thoughts tumbling through his head. If the munitions hold were penetrated, the ship would be blown sky high. As Master of the ship, he'd be responsible for the loss of all these men. Their lives depended on his decision.

He ran his fingers over his short hair, rested his elbows on the wheel, and cradled his head in his hands. Had he chosen the best chance for survival? His mind raced through the options once more. If they were discovered by the Japs, would they be able to fight them off?

Was it possible they might stand a better chance of coming through this by hiding on the island? If he had made the wrong decision, how many children back home might be left fatherless?

He was glad no one had mentioned surrender. That was simply an option he wouldn't even discuss. The news he'd received just before the ship had left New Guinea . . . that he'd become a father . . . flashed in his mind. His wife had just delivered their first child — a boy. Would he ever see his son?

He slapped his hand against the wheel. "Cut it out, Robert Daly. We're all going to get out of this mess! We're gonna get off these rocks! Get your butt in gear! You have a job to do!"

Lieutenant Wagner rested his elbows on the rail of the starboard bridge wing as he meticulously searched the tree-lined beach with his binoculars. He'd seen no sign of the enemy yet, but he couldn't help feeling they'd show up before long. He jerked his head around when he heard his name called on his sound system.

"Lieutenant . . . this is Cramer in tub seven. There's a small boat coming down the coast heading directly at us. I'd say it's a mile or two away. You'd better take a closer look through your binoculars, see if you can tell if it's friendly."

Wagner jogged across the bridge and out onto the port-side wing.

Looking up at gun tub seven, he saw Cramer pointing in the direction of a bobbing object. He lifted his field glasses to take a closer look. It looked like a small fishing boat, definitely headed their way. Since he didn't have his phone system hooked up right here, he yelled so that Cramer could hear him. "I see it. Doesn't look much bigger than one of our lifeboats. It's probably just a Filipino fisherman, but we're gonna have to make sure. I'll be right up."

Captain Daly strode onto the port wing. "What's going on?"

Wagner pointed to the approaching boat.

Daly took a look through his binoculars. "What do you suppose they're up to?"

Wagner continued to watch the small craft. "I don't know, but I don't like it. Could be just a local fisherman and his family . . . but there's also the remote chance there are Japs on board."

The skipper dropped his glasses and shrugged. "Even if there are, what harm could they do? They don't seem to have any heavy guns, and they're not about to board us."

Wagner didn't answer right away. He slowly lowered his binoculars, his eyes steady on the Captain's. "Suppose it is Japs, and they have a medium-sized aerial bomb with it's detonator on its nose. If that were mounted somewhere on their bow, either on their deck or worse . . . on a log under water . . . can you imagine what could happen?"

Daly gravely nodded. "I see what you're getting at."

"Let's exaggerate even further. Let's say they approach, smiling all the way . . . maybe even waving tiny American flags . . . and ram us with that little tub. Ka *BOOM*! We suddenly have a hole at the water line on our port side big enough to drive a truck through." He cocked his head to one side as he lifted his eyebrows. "Think back. They tried that in Leyte against one of the Navy ships after the invasion. They weren't successful, but they did try it. Remember?"

The Captain lowered his binoculars. A stunned expression crossed his face as he recalled the incident. "You're right. Those sneaky little buggers are capable of doing something like that." He licked his lower lip. "What are we going to do about it?"

Wagner frowned. "Although that last scenario is very remote, we're taking no chances. We'll have to chase them out of here before they get much closer." He turned away. "I'm going up to the flying bridge, and I'm taking the trumpet with me. I'll get Martinez to talk to them when they're close enough to hear." A sly grin shaped his lips. "He can give them the General MacArthur routine he gave the kids. It worked once. Let's see if it will work again."

Wagner climbed the ladder and found Martinez in gun tub four on the starboard side. After explaining the problem confronting them, and outlining what he wanted the gunner to do, Martinez nodded. Unhooking the straps, he removed himself from the gunner's position. The loader, Hathaway, strapped himself into the shooter's harness, as Wagner and Martinez walked over to the port-side rail.

By this time the engine of the small craft could be heard as it chugged toward the *Albert A.*

Martinez laughed. "My God, listen to that thing. It must have a 'one-lunger' that's missing every fourth or fifth stroke."

The roar was escaping from the unmuffled one-cylinder engine, with its large, two-foot diameter fly wheel that kept the motor from stalling.

Wagner looked around. All the men he could see wore wide grins as they watched the approaching antiquated trawler. He heard one mutter, "That thing should be in the Smithsonian. The engine must have been made before the turn of the century."

Several men snickered.

Two scantily dressed individuals, wearing nothing but what looked like large diapers, stepped out of the small-wheel cabin and waved.

Wagner placed the speaking trumpet in the hands of Martinez. "Give them orders to clear the area. I don't want them coming any closer."

The gunner took the horn and raised it to his mouth. "Do not approach our ship. This is an order from General Douglas MacArthur. Leave the area immediately." He repeated the order in Spanish, twice.

The two individuals on the ship waved and yelled something.

"What are they saying, Martinez?"

"I can't understand because I can't hear them. There's too much noise coming from below with all that clanking steel on the deck and the winch steam noise. They're not stopping or turning, Sir. Whadda ya want me to do?"

Wagner watched the smiles disappear from the faces of the watching crew as the missing motor increased its rpm.

"Damn!"

The boat not only hadn't turned away, it hurried to meet them. He turned to tub seven. "Cramer! Call back aft to Williams on the big gun.

Have him pull out an M-l rifle from the munitions locker, put a full clip in it, and stand by ready to fire if I give him the word."

Martinez, shifting from foot to foot, picked up the trumpet again. "Should I make my message a bit stronger, Lieutenant?"

"Shit, yes! Let them know we'll sink them if they come any closer."

The gunner rattled off his Spanish in a forceful tone. There could be no doubt of his message to the crew of the dilapidated old fishing boat.

Wagner, watching the approaching vessel through his binoculars, suddenly sucked in an audible deep breath. "Oh hell, look what just came out of the cabin. He couldn't be more than ten or twelve years old. Geeze, a kid on board that tub. That's all we need."

The gunner strapped into the 20mm cannon to Wagner's right offered a suggestion. "I could put a couple rounds right along side their boat, Sir. They'd get the message then, I'm sure."

Wagner nodded. "I thought of that, but the noise from your gun could wake up some nearby Japs, letting them know we're here. The longer we can delay that, the better." He rubbed a hand over his eyes. "We may have to resort to your gun if the smaller, quieter M-1 doesn't stop them." His eyes narrowed. "If those guys should dive over the side and start swimming for shore, we'll use your gun to sink the damn boat . . . kid or no kid."

The voices from the small boat could now be heard as it continued toward the *Albert A.* In perfect English they shouted, "We need food! We need food!"

Captain Daly moved to Wagner's side. "What do you think? Could they be Japs, or are they just Filipino fishermen?"

"I don't know, and I don't care. We're in a war and we're stuck on an enemy-held island. I'm not taking any chances." He walked over to tub seven, took the headset from Cramer, and spoke into it. "Williams?"

"Yes, Sir."

"Try not to hit anyone, but put a round into that boat's bow."

"Will do, Sir." Twenty seconds later the M-1 spoke. Wood splinters flew from the bowsprit area. The figures on the boat hit the deck when they heard the bullet strike their vessel.

"Do it again, Williams," shouted Wagner as he watched closely through his binoculars. "I want there to be no doubt in their minds we mean business."

A second shot found its mark. More splinters flew into the air.

Within seconds, though no one could be seen, the boat turned west toward the open sea and chugged away.

Captain Daly looked directly at Wagner. "What ya think? Were they Japs or Filipinos?"

Wagner pushed his jaw out. "Does it matter?" He grinned. "Ten to one they're Filipino, but it's that one in ten I wasn't willing to chance." He turned toward the number seven tub. "Cramer, keep your eye on them until they're out of sight."

The young gunner nodded. "Yes, Sir."

Wagner looked once more at the small boat before following the Captain back to the bridge deck. He watched them throw out their fishing nets off the after-end of their boat and half smiled. "Make those odds more like a hundred to one they're Filipinos, but my job is to save our butts, not feed our hungry allies."

"You're right, of course, and you made the right decision." Captain Daly turned and climbed down the ladder to the bridge deck, followed by Lieutenant Wagner.

Chapter 6

CAPTAIN DALY strode to his quarters next to the chart room. For the last seven hours, because of the heat and the ship's situation, he'd been clothed only in his cutoffs and slippers, which he had hurriedly donned after he'd learned of the current catastrophe. Now, as Master of the ship, he decided it would be proper to dress in khaki shirt and pants before checking on the preparedness of the ship and crew. They needed to see him standing straight and confident, an attitude cutoffs couldn't convey. He ran a comb through his short hair, took one last look in the mirror, and marched out of the room.

He trotted down the two inside ladders from his quarters. Looking in the galley, he spotted the Chief Cook standing over the large,

coal-fired stove. The man had done a first-rate job of keeping the hands fed with warm soup and coffee while they labored.

"Is the Bully Beef going to hold up, Cookie? And if it won't, what else do you have that can nourish the boys?" He opened the Dutch door and walked into the over 100-degree area. "How about some turkey with all the trimmings?"

The Aussie Chief Cook, known to everyone on board as Cookie, stood no more than five feet tall, a lovable little liar who enjoyed entertaining anyone who would listen to his wild, unbelievable stories. He delighted in recounting imaginative tales of his wartime heroism in the Solomon Islands invasion. He looked up quickly, appearing slightly startled by the Captain's words. "No, Sir, we jus' give out the las' order, but 'ow about some Myaine lobster?" His strong, Outback accent sometimes made understanding him difficult.

Both men chuckled. The availability of either of those foods didn't exist, and they knew it. The *Albert A.* had been out of everything but powdered eggs, dehydrated potatoes, and diced beets for the last three weeks — that is, until the Steward had been able to score 140 cases of canned Australian bully beef at the last stop at Orr Bay, New Guinea. The crew jokingly referred to it as ground-up mountain goat that had died of old age, but grudgingly admitted it was better than no meat at all.

"'elp yerself, Cap'n, to my Bully Beef Borscht." With the ladle he held in his hand, Cookie pointed to a stainless steel stew pot sitting on the stove. "Cups is right over there." He again pointed with the ladle.

"I already had some. It wasn't bad." Captain Daly held up his hand in acknowledgment. "In fact, it tasted pretty good. Your young Philippine helper, Raul, brought some up to me. Is it one of your name creations, or cooking masterpieces . . . or both?"

"Aye, Cap'n, it's both." A wide grin creased his face. "An' it'll bloody well put 'air on yer chest, too."

The Captain dipped a cup into the thick soup. "Then I guess I'd better have some more. Mrs. Daly complains I don't have enough hair on my chest . . . or on my head." He shook the drips off the cup before bringing it to his mouth to take a sip. "Where are all your helpers?"

"The Steward put 'em all to work. Some are running steel, and learning to be gunners. My Second Cook has been made a medic. Raul is keeping busy running BBB and coffee out to the work gangs." While he talked, Cookie hoisted a sack of dehydrated potatoes over his shoulder and poured half of it into an over-sized pot of boiling water. "Me . . . why I'm jus' goofin' off down 'ere, enjoyin' this toasty warm stove and the balmy 106 degree weather, and lookin' for somethin' to do." The sweat dripping off his face as he bustled about the galley belied his seemingly cheerful words.

Everyone, the Captain included, loved Cookie's sense of humor, and his ability to tell the outrageous stories about fighting Japs in the Solomon Islands with the Australian army.

Captain Daly smiled inwardly. The little man must have spent his daytime hours dreaming up the far-fetched tales he regaled the crew with in the evenings. They were always full of blood and guts, with him the conquering hero. His prowess, and the circumstances surrounding the incidents, were so completely unbelievable that no one, except maybe a Captain Marvel could have achieved them. The real fun though, was to see this barely five-foot man, who couldn't have weighed more than a hundred pounds soaking wet, cavorting on a hatch cover. With leaps and bounds and flailing arms, he described his hand-to-hand combat with the Japs.

To all the men on board, it was pure entertainment, the only kind they had. Merchant ships had no movies or USO shows. The men had to resort to their own devices for relaxation. And Cookie had the ability to make his shipmates laugh with his wild stories. It took very little to entertain the men, and entertain he certainly did.

Before the convoy had headed out to the invasion point, the *Albert A. Robinson* had swung for 92 days on the hook at Hollandia, New Guinea. On many occasions during that time, Cookie would have 15 or more individuals at once rolling with laughter on the number four hatch cover as he unloaded a grisly episode of his heroism. Always, when he had finished a wild tale, he'd raise his right hand as if taking an oath, declaring, "And that's the bloody truth, mates, every bloody word of it." But the twinkle in his eye and the upturned corners of his lips left little doubt he was a masterful, creative story-teller.

The Captain had heard secondhand one of Cookie's outrageous stories, and decided to have a bit of fun with it. Maintaining a serious expression, he asked, "Cookie, do you remember a couple of weeks ago, while we were in New Guinea, you told a bunch of the guys about a battle you were involved in down in the Solomons? I think you said you were up to your ankles in blood, with dead Japs all around you. More were attacking, climbing over the bodies of their dead comrades to get to you. All you had to defend yourself was your strength, your courage, and a large machete. Do you remember?"

The puzzled expression on the little man's face almost made the Captain laugh, but he managed to keep his face solemn.

"Aye . . . I 'member." Confusion clouded his eyes. He clearly had no idea what the Old Man might be driving at.

Captain Daly continued. "Well, I was wondering, if the Japs do attack us from the beach, would you be willing to . . . you know . . . show us how to defend ourselves? Lieutenant Wagner would sure appreciate any help you can pass on to him and his men. You know, the Armed Guard are not trained in hand-to-hand combat."

A strained smile struggled to appear on Cookie's face. He took in a big breath of air, then burst into laughter. "Ha, ha. Oh, that's a bloody good one, Captain. For a minute there I almost thought you were serious." He wiped his eyes. "Ha, ha!"

A loud chuckle escaped from the Captain, too, as he put his empty cup in the sink. He turned to face the little cook, but his expression turned serious. "Keep up the good work, Cookie. You've done a great job of creating meals for us out of the meager supplies you have left." Captain Daly smiled, turned, and walked out of the room.

Ten steps down the companionway he came upon the officer's mess hall, being readied as the temporary infirmary. Doc Johnson and Elijah busily tore sheets into two-inch strips and wound them up to be used as bandages, another commodity they were short of.

Elijah, a massive black man, might have been good-looking if it hadn't been for an ugly, unstitched scar a half-inch wide that looped across his cheek and under his chin. His bulging right bicep bore several more wide, three-inch scars, the result of untreated knife wounds. Elijah got the wounds, so the story went, in a knife fight one night during his days as a gang leader in Harlem. When the fight ended, Elijah was bleeding profusely from the cuts he had sustained, and the members of his gang carried their semi-conscious leader to his mother's tenement apartment. After telling her what had happened, they quickly left, still fearing reprisals from the rival gang, who had lost their leader in the fight.

Afraid of what the police might do to her son, and with no money and no insurance, Elijah's mother turned to a neighbor down the hall who served as a midwife in that poverty-stricken area. The woman took one look at Elijah and the blood-soaked sheets on which he lay and threw up her hands. "He won't live through the night. He'll be dead by morning." She'd walked away shaking her head.

Desperate, and with nowhere else to turn, a barely conscious Elijah and his mother prayed. He made a promise that night. If Jesus would save his worthless hide this one more time, Elijah would devote his life to spreading the Word of God, and His Son, Jesus . . . and he'd kept his word.

He told the hair-raising details of that life-changing night to anyone who would listen, his eyes glistening with the fervor of his faith. Captain Daly had heard the story directly from Elijah's lips and felt the black man's dedication. Being a firm believer in the old adage "There are no atheists in a foxhole under fire," the Captain knew, without a doubt, that Elijah would be invaluable to Doc if the ship came under attack.

He stepped into the room. "How're things going?"

Both men looked his way and gave him a thumbs-up sign. Doc answered, his customary cigarette flapping in the middle of his mouth as he talked. "We're as ready as we can be with what they provide us. We've robbed all the medical supplies the Armed Guard had back aft, and scrounged through the ship, confiscating any type of antiseptic we could find. We even swiped the medical supplies and first-aid kits from the lifeboats." He made a sweeping gesture toward the makeshift dispensary. "What you see is what we got . . . period."

Captain Daly shook his head as he scanned the limited supplies assembled on one of the four tables in the room. "Pitiful!" He rubbed the back of his neck. "If we do come under attack, you'd better make sure Cookie has boiling water available for sterilizing the needles. You may need to sew up a gash or two . . . or anything else that might need it."

Chief Steward Hogan bustled through the door, his arms crammed with bedding. "Here you go, Doc. This is the last of the blankets and sheets. Where do you want them?" A look of surprise covered his face when he peeked around the tall load in his arms. "Oh . . . hi, Captain."

The round-faced, portly built Steward, brought a smile to the Captain's face. He'd surmised Hogan must have been 4F, like Elijah, and exempt from the draft. The Steward possessed the flattest feet imaginable, so flat they made him walk on his heels and waddle like a duck.

So many men in the Merchant Marine were like that, unable to pass

Armed Forces physicals. But if a man wanted to serve his country, age or shortcomings like these made no difference aboard ship. You could always sail with the Merchant Marine as long as you could do the job. Captain Daly respected those men.

He took another quick survey of the room. "Hey, Doc," he pointed to a corner table, "I see you have only three mattresses here." He turned to Hogan. "Is that all the spares we have?"

Hogan shrugged. "That's it, Captain."

Daly again rubbed the back of his neck. They were bound to need more than that if things got bad. He closed his eyes, his mind running through the available options.

"Doc, why don't you and Hogan snag one mattress off the bunk beds in each room in the deck-hands quarters? They aren't going to need both of them. No more than one will be sleeping at any given time. Hell — until we get off this damn island, it's doubtful anyone will be sleeping." He frowned. If they weren't able to back the ship off at high tide, they'd more than likely come under attack, and then no one would sleep. He shuddered. Doc would need a lot more mattresses if that happened.

Doc set the strip he'd been winding down on a table. "If this thing gets as ugly as Wagner thinks it might, we'll definitely need more places where guys can be laid out. We have the four bunks in the hospital room. We'll use those for casualties that can be left alone. The ones we have to watch closely will be in here. We'll definitely need more mattresses to lay them on." He looked around the room. "Come on, Hogan. It looks like we have space for three of four more."

Captain Daly, opened his mouth to say something, then paused as Tony Ratto, an Oiler from the Black Gang below, squished his way into the room. His shoes, soaked with his sweat, left damp footprints with each step. His shorts, the only clothes he wore, dripped wherever he stood. His gaze fastened on Doc. "Dere you are. Da Chief sent me up to get some salt pills. Da engine room is too hot. We gotta have some salt pills. Guys are keeling over from da heat."

"I've got some right here, Tony." He grabbed a large jar off the table and handed it to the dripping Oiler. "Tony," he shook his finger to make his point, "make sure everyone takes one every hour, and that you all drink plenty of water." He tapped the dripping man on the chest. "You got that? . . . Drink lots of water." Doc looked at Tony's shoes and shook his head. He could imagine how hot it must be down below.

Tony nodded vigorously. "You ain't never been hot like it is down there today. It makes yuh understand your fear of hell!" He lifted the jar. "Tanks for the pills." Not one for conversation, unless it was about the chicken farm he hoped to own one day, Tony turned and squished his way out of the room.

Captain Daly's stomach churned. "Those poor devils. With the live steam and the heat from the fire box, that place must be like a sauna turned up to maximum." He unbuttoned his khaki shirt and ballooned it a couple times to draw in some air. "I'm sweating like a hound right here! But I think I'm about to learn what really hot is. I'm heading for the engine room next." He waved his shirt again, trying to cool his body. "Full tide will be here in about an hour. I've got high hopes we're going to get off this rock pile — that is, if the Chief can get me power by then."

Elijah smiled, his resonant drawl spilling out in deep tones. "We's pr'yin' for that to happen, Cap'n."

The Captain slapped him on the back. "I guess we all are, Elijah, but I want you especially to keep right on praying." A half-smile curved his lips. "I think the Lord will listen more to prayers from you than from the rest of us." He started out the door, but stopped and turned in the doorway. "Don't forget to get those extra mattresses, Doc.

Doc paused to light up a new cigarette. "What say you give me a hand, Hogan. We can get it done right now."

Captain Daly followed Tony's sweaty footprints down the companionway to the rear of the midship housing where the entrance to the engine room stood. As he stepped in, a blast of hot air hit him. He found it hard to draw in enough air to breathe. This was not a place he wanted to be, but he forced himself to start the climb down the four floors to the engine room main deck. Remembering Tony's last words brought back memories of his childhood Sunday School, where the teacher had impressed on young minds the discomforts of hell. This hell-hole he now found himself in had live steam in it. The temperature had to be at least 120 degrees. The humidity, almost 100 percent, made it difficult to breathe.

He looked around. Men, still in their makeshift scaffolds, busily worked at making final repairs. One hung in a Bosun's chair right over the main boiler while he torqued down a large clamp. They all had stripped down to their skivvies. Their bodies glistened with sweat as if they'd been dunked in a pool of fine oil.

He paused. He'd come down three flights and already his uniform was soaked. Even though he'd left his shirt hanging loose, the heat was taking its toll. He spotted the Chief just below him. Leaning his upper body over the iron banister, he called to him.

The Chief Engineer looked up. "Aye, Captain. Ve fired her up over an hour ago. The boys have done a good job. Everything seems to be holding at the moment, but ve von't know for sure until ve get up full steam." He lapsed into a coughing fit. The man couldn't seem to manage more than a few sentences without that happening.

Captain Daly, seeing the redness in the old-timer's face as he struggled for air in the stifling heat, hesitated to ask the obvious question. He waited for the coughing to stop. When it had, he shouted down, "How long will that be, Chief?"

"Another two-and-a-half hours. All my boys wore gloves and ve vorked the pipes hot so I could keep hot vater in the boiler."

Two-and-a-half hours? He didn't want to hear that. "It's almost noon right now. I need full steam in one hour."

Frustrated, the Chief glared back with fire in his eyes. "Vell, vy don't you come on down here and see if you can turn the knob a little bit higher in the fire box than vat ve can."

"All right, all right, you crusty old Scandahoovian square-head." The Captain couldn't help but smile. The 68-year-old salty Swede had given up his comfortable retirement to help the war effort with his considerable knowledge of marine steam engines. He was to be admired. "Let the wheel-house know the second you have enough steam to turn the screw over."

The Chief touched three fingers of his right hand to his forehead. "Vell, maybe in two hours . . . if you're a good boy."

The Captain returned the salute with a wave of his hand. Before he turned to leave he shouted, "Every minute's important, Chief."

"Aye," snapped the Chief, "As if I didn't know that."

Daly made his way up and out of the inferno of the engine room. The companionway suddenly seemed cool . . . even comfortable. He looked back at the heat waves coming out of the door he'd just exited and shook his head. Those poor devils, he thought, they must really think they're in hell.

He rounded the corner away from the heat. It was time to check on the removal of the metal mats from the number three hold, he told himself. Exiting the midship housing on the starboard side of the ship, he approached the hub of activity on deck.

Boats, the Bosun, had the two winches and their thick cables humming as they descended into the hold. The team below hurriedly wrapped them around the next nested load and signaled a double thumbs-up. Then Boats set the machinery in motion, with an upward jerk on the two levers, custom-carved two-by-fours fashioned by Chips, the Ship's Carpenter, so one man could work both winches. The cables tightened, singing as they vibrated with the strain on the metallic fibers. The heavy load slowly raised from the depths, swung away from the hold, then lowered with a clanking crash onto the deck.

"You'd think you guys have been doing this job all your lives," shouted the Captain over the clattering noise.

A couple of deck hands acknowledged his compliment with an "OK" gesture, then quickly unhooked the cable wrap.

"Stand clear!" Boats' voice carried over the clanks and bangs of the desperate work going on. Steam chugged from the two large winch engines. He pulled up on the jerry-rigged handles that controlled the windings of the cables and the long metal lines snapped into the air from under the metal bundles. They rose up off the deck, and like a professional diver, plunged into the hold for the next load.

"You're a natural, Boats," the Captain shouted. He realized the old, bearded Bosun couldn't hear him. The hiss of escaping steam from the winch engines would have drowned out his words. He gave him a thumbs-up signal instead.

Boats returned the gesture as soon as the cables hit the bottom of the hold, ready for the next load to be attached.

The Captain answered with a wave. His crew was doing one hell of a job, better than he'd thought possible by these inexperienced cargo handlers. They had come through like veterans.

Daly made his way forward under the gun tub on the bow that held the 3-inch/50 cannon, intent on viewing the rocks that held the *Albert A. Robinson* a prisoner. He leaned over the rail, his brow knit together. No rocks showed above the surface, but through the crystal clear water he could see the ominous monsters some 10 to 20 feet below. He shuddered. Might those jagged hunks become the headstones for his beloved Liberty ship and her crew?

He looked at the now clear blue sky. His eyes drifted shut. A silent prayer formed in his head. His lips moved as he whispered words of thanks for the efficiency of his crew and the safety they'd already received. He gripped the railing and raised a fervent request for further help and protection. No doubt about it, he thought, there are no atheists when you're under fire . . . or possibly about to be. He smacked the railing once with his fist, then returned to the midship housing, this time on the port side.

Daly made his way back aft to number five hold, the one filled with munitions. As he approached, the clanging and banging of steel landing on steel assaulted his ears. He stood off to the side watching the teamwork of his exhausted, bedraggled crew. Ivan and his team of assemblers took the steel sheet from the men carting it up the starboard side. Men on the deck lifted it to the men on top, who slid it over to be latched with the previous plate. As fast as one had been fastened in place, another team of men delivered a new one.

The noise here rivaled that at the number three hold. He had to yell to be heard. "How's it coming, Ivan?"

Ivan looked down from the top of the pile. "It's going good, Captain. We've passed seven feet high. Now we're heading for eight. That should stop most anything from penetrating this hold."

"When you've reached the eight-foot on the hatch cover, start lacing those babies on the deck. Five to six feet of steel all around number five would make me feel a lot safer." He cupped his hands around his mouth as he shouted so his words would carry up to his Third Mate. "We'll want to layer all the way around the mast house, too. That'll give us more protection and more weight back aft. That's the name of the game!"

"Will do, Captain. We were planning to stack those plates all around the deck, and also back aft. As long as they keep coming, we'll keep stacking." Ivan put both his hands in the small of his back just about where his kidneys should be, and leaned back, stretching into an arch. "Thank God, the 'tween deck of number three hold is the smallest cargo area on the ship."

Captain Daly looked at his watch and frowned. "You know, Ivan, it's possible we'll be able to make another attempt to free ourselves from the rocks in an hour or two." He chewed the corner of his lower lip. "With that in mind, why don't you and your gang start loading around the edges now. Seven feet of layered steel on the hatch cover itself should be enough protection. Let's start spreading some on the surrounding deck."

Ivan nodded. "Sounds good to me." He turned to his awaiting crew. "You heard him, guys. Let's get started on the port side first."

"Keep up the good work." Captain Daly whirled around and started back toward the midship housing, his mind struggling for solutions to the predicament of his grounded ship. Had he done everything possible to enhance their next attempt to free her? The weight forward had been lessened. The water tanks had been emptied and the cargo shifted aft. What else could he do? Or would that be enough?

Once again he remembered the anchors. He hadn't forgotten about the anchors. They had talked about them earlier, but dismissed the idea of lowering them, in case they'd hang up in the rocks. But, if they just dropped one, with all its chain, and cut it free, it would be a worthwhile load to get rid of.

Chapter 7

CAPTAIN DALY broke into a trot. "Cash! Josh!" he yelled as he entered the midship housing. "Wherever you are, I need one of you in the wheel-house, *NOW!*"

Josh's voice drifted down from the chart room. "I'm already here, Captain."

He clambered up the inside ladder, two steps at a time and burst through the door into the wheel-house. Struggling to get enough air, he bent over and put his hands on his knees. "I want you — to lower — one of the anchors, plus all of its chain." He pulled more air into his lungs. "That should take several tons of weight off the bow." Still bent over, he took one more deep breath, then dropped his hands from his knees and stood up straight. "That's where we need to lose it most . . . right there on the bow."

Josh licked his lips. By the look in his eye, the Captain could tell the idea was playing around in his head. "That's a good idea, if the anchor happens to fall on the right side of those big rocks we're nestled into." He rubbed his hand over his short hair. "But I thought we scotched that. You'd said it wasn't worth the gamble. It might become wedged between the rocks and we'd be stuck like a dog on a leash tied to a tree."

The Captain smiled. "I know we already decided against it, but I have a different plan."

Josh raised his eyebrows. "And that is?"

"I want you to lower one of the anchors and its chain. Then we'll cut the chain and let it go to the bottom. Hell, if we don't get off these rocks soon, we won't have any use for the damn thing anyway."

Josh frowned thoughtfully. "If we can find a way to cut through that thick chain, that's a darn good idea."

The Captain jerked his head up. "We'll find a way! I'm sure the engine room has hacksaws, or something we can use."

Josh scruffed the underside of his chin with the backs of the fingers of his right hand. "I wonder if the engine room has an acetylene torch. If they do, we could cut the chain with the torch."

Daly smiled. "Good . . . good idea. Call the engine room. See if they have a torch and enough acetylene to cut one of those monster links." He wiped away the stinging sweat that had run into his eyes. "It would be my guess they'd have to make two complete cuts to get through the two and a half inches of forged steel. That's a pretty substantial amount of cutting."

Josh crossed to the talking tube in five quick steps. He blew hard into it. The whistle sounded in the depths of the ship that was the engine room.

The Second Engineer, Svenson, answered the call.

Josh explained why they needed a torch when they lowered the anchor. "We'd let out the whole length of chain, then cut the damn thing loose."

"We got a little tank down here. You know how to cut metal?"

Josh chuckled. "Svenson, I haven't the foggiest idea. You got someone down there that could give me a hand?"

"You're in luck. Crosby, First Engineer, is an expert. I'll send him up with the tank and torch. Meet him at the entrance to the engine room."

"Thanks, Svenson." Josh turned to the Captain to report the results of the conversation.

Daly held up his hand before Josh could speak. "I heard. Get going."

Josh scurried out the door. As he slid down the first ladder he thought about Bob Crosby. The poor devil had become pretty much a loner since he had received that "Dear John" letter from his beautiful wife of three years. His marriage had apparently had problems, but they all came to a head when he insisted they wait to have children until the war ended.

She'd wanted to try to get pregnant on his last shore leave, but he'd refused. This had led to a verbal battle royal, one they hadn't had time to smooth over before he had to ship out. His first letter after leaving San Francisco reached him in New Guinea, with her request for a divorce. It really hit him hard.

Josh scrambled down a second ladder to get to the main deck, still thinking about Crosby. What a rotten thing to have happen. Since then, Crosby had spent most of his off-duty time in his quarters, riding his stationary bike and having bouts of crying. He often showed up for chow with red nose and eyes. All the officers felt sorry for the poor man, but there wasn't anything they could do to help him.

Josh rounded the corner as Crosby stepped out of the inferno of the engine room. It seemed to Josh the handsome, muscular man appeared to be looking a bit better than he had in the past week or two. Maybe the chaos of the last hours had taken his mind off his troubles.

Crosby stretched out his dripping arms. Puddles of sweat formed where his shoes stood on the deck. "Oh, wow. So this is what the real world feels like!" He took a deep breath and smiled, the first smile Josh had seen from him since the letter. "Or is this heaven? I know it's hell down there." He pointed at the engine room below.

"Man, it must be miserable for you poor suckers." Josh indicated the entrance to the engine room. He looked more closely at Crosby. "Where's the tank and the torch?"

The First Engineer shook his head. "I left it below. When I went to get it I remembered there's not enough gas in it to cut a half-inch chain, much less a double cut on a two and a half incher." A sheepish grin crept onto his face. "I wanted an excuse to get out of that hell hole for a couple of minutes," he leaned his head toward the engine room door, "so I came up to give you the bad news."

"I can't say I blame you, but now we have the problem of getting the weight of one of those anchors off the bow. How's your supply of hacksaws . . . and new blades?"

"Josh, I was thinking coming up the ladders, if my memory of physics is correct, by just putting those cast-iron anchors in the water, you'll reduce their weight by twenty-five or thirty percent. Since those suckers weigh more than several tons each, that's a lot of weight you'd be removing from the bow."

"Hey, that's a good thought. If you can get me some steam, I —"

Crosby put up his hand. "Hold it, Josh, hear me out. I think you might like this even better." He took in a lungful of air and let it out slowly. "Chips or the Mate will have to confirm this, but I think I saw a toggle pin at the end of the chain in the fore-peak chain locker the last time I worked on the hoist in the fo'c'sle. If it's removed, it would allow the chain to be free when it reaches the end."

"Whoa! Wait a minute. Chips knows all about this?"

"Yeah. He assists the Mate by handling the anchor brakes when the anchor is lowered into the water, and retracting it when needs be." Crosby made a motion, as if he was pulling a pin. "You yank that toggle pin, and it lets the chain release. Then, out the hawse-pipe it goes, kerplunk, into the water." He smiled. "Once you've jettisoned one anchor and all its chain, you could lower the other one into the water just deep enough to release about twenty-five percent of its weight, too."

"Oh, the Captain will love this." Josh rubbed his sweaty palms together. "I'll chase down Chips. He'll probably be glad to be relieved of working on those metal plates. We'll go up to the fo'c'sle and start lowering one of those weighty monsters." He scratched his head. "Will she just unload herself with gravity, or will we need steam?"

Crosby moved to the door leading to the engine room. "You'd only need steam to pull her up. She'll let go by herself. Now, I've got to get back below." He stuck his head in the doorway and stepped back from the blast of heat that greeted him. He took one last lungful of unheated air. "The Chief is on a wild tear to get our boilers up to full steam in record time." With a half grin on his face, he shook his head. "And by God, I think that old Swedish Merlin . . . the Wizard of Steam . . . is actually going to do it."

"See ya." He waved his hand as he stepped through the opening.

Josh waved at the departing Engineer. He stuck his head through the opening. "Thanks for the ideas," he shouted to Crosby, who had started his descent.

Josh found Chips near the number three hold, soaked with sweat. He'd been lugging the landing plates back aft since 0430 that morning. When Josh outlined what needed to be done, a broad smile creased the face of the Ship's Carpenter. The speed with which the tall man turned over the hauling job to someone else brought a grin to Josh's face.

Usually very bashful because of his severe case of the stutters, Chips struggled to get out his words. "I'll b-b-be g-g-glad to do it, J-J-Josh. I'm s-so h-h-happy t-t-to g-get rid of that j-job." He pulled off the heavy gloves he wore to cart the sharp metal, and stuffed them in the back of his pants.

"Will it work, releasing an anchor?" Josh asked as they strode forward.

"D-don't see why n-not." Chips seldom spoke any more than he had to, acutely conscious of his speech impediment, but it certainly didn't interfere with his ability to create complex structures to secure cargoes, or build scaffolds, cat walks, or intricate cabinets to house objects of all types.

They reached the bow and peered over the rail at the rocks that held the ship in place. "There, l-look at that one." On the port side of the ship, right under the anchor, Chips pointed out a large rock with a broad crown that appeared to be higher than the others. "We can l-l-lower the port-side anchor onto that one, actually r-rest the h-hook on it. Th-that will g-get rid of *all* of its weight, n-n-not just twenty-five p-p-percent"

Josh nodded. "If we lower it only until it rests on the rock, we can't get into any trouble if the anchor should move."

Chips agreed with a nod of his head. "You watch. T-t-tell me when it's in p-place." He went down to the fo'c'sle where the chain locker and the mechanism for raising and lowering the anchors were kept.

Josh hung over the bow railing, watching the anchor slowly descend into the crystal-clear water. When he saw the first indication of slack in the chain he hollered to Chips. "It's in place!" He made his way to the fo'c'sle in time to watch Chips drop the starboard anchor, pull the toggle pin that held the chain firm, and watch it all slide out the hawse pipe.

Together, the two men went back to the bow and viewed their handiwork.

Josh slapped Chips on the back. "Good job, man!"

Chips grinned. "That should g-g-get a lot of weight off the b-bow." He took a deep breath, his shoulders sagging as he let it out. "G-guess I'd better get b-back to hauling m-metal." He yanked the gloves out of his pants and stalked away.

Josh jogged double-time to the bridge to report to Captain Daly.

The Captain's eyebrows drew together when he heard what the two men had done. "Are you sure the anchor resting on the rock can't topple off and become wedged?"

"Not a chance. If it were to slip to one side or another off the rock it's on, it would simply swing in the water because it can't go any lower." Josh shrugged his shoulders. "Chips braked the chain securely . . . very securely. He assured me it can't slip or let out any more chain."

"Good. That's another load of weight off the bow. At the moment I can't think of any more we can get rid of." Balling his hands into fists, he shook them in the direction of the communicator tubes. "Come on, engine room, get me some steam!"

Captain Daly paced the deck of the wheel-house. For what must have been the twentieth time in the last ten minutes he glanced at the clock on the wall. It read 1330, an hour and a half since noon. No word had come from the engine room yet, and full tide had been half an hour ago. Soon it would start to ebb, and their chance to get free would be gone.

Just about the time he was ready to call below, he heard the whistle from the engine room communicator. He rushed to the tube. "This is the Captain — please give me some good news!"

"Vell, all leaks are holding for the moment. You can give her full astern." The Captain had to wait while the Chief hacked and coughed. "But stay within earshot of the communications tube in case I have to shut her down."

The Captain snapped the tube closed and yanked the brass mechanical indicator into the full-astern position. Bells rang as he slapped it back and forth twice. He grabbed the speaking trumpet and strode out onto the bridge wing. Facing the stern he called, "First Mate Cash, I need you on the bridge immediately." He actually wanted a helmsman, but didn't want to announce that information for all to hear until he was sure the engine would perform.

Standing still, his head cocked to one side, he listened for the sound and the feel of the engine. He prayed a "*Thank you*" when the throbbing of the big, three-cylinder steam engine made its presence felt. The six, 20-foot stanchion rocker arms began to rotate up and down in the engine room; the large, four-bladed propeller started to turn. His ship once again had power. He breathed a relieved sigh.

Silence fell over the ship as all work ceased. Tension seemed to crackle in the air. About 30 seconds later, someone yelled "Yea!" followed by shouts of success from almost every man on board. Everyone had a grin on his face. The old Liberty ship trembled, as if being throttled by mother nature. The screw's rotation increased, faster and faster, as the 2,500 horsepower reciprocating steam engine gave every bit of energy it could muster to free the ship.

The *Albert A.* continued to shiver and shake for 20 minutes. The wide grins slowly disappeared on the faces of the crew, replaced with the tight-lipped realization that the ship was stuck worse than anyone had imagined. Gloom filled the air.

Captain Daly shook his head, disappointment eating away at his insides. It appeared now their only chance of survival rested with the two LSTs. He wasn't even sure they were big enough to drag the ship from its prison. Good Lord, he thought, we can't even make another attempt to get free until two in the morning, at the next full tide. He didn't hold out much hope that the LSTs would have enough power to tow the *Albert A.* free when they arrived at 1700 hours that afternoon.

He frowned. His shoulders drooped. He had pinned his hopes on being able to back off the rocks. And now that that wasn't going to happen, there was no choice but to prepare for the worst. He had to face facts. They were hung up on the rocks on a heavily armed, Japanese-controlled island. To hope that the ship wouldn't be discovered before help arrived was a rather thin thread to hang one's future on. Being prepared was their best defense — all that could save them now.

He trudged across the room. He grasped the engine room speaking tube and blew hard.

The craggy old voice of the Chief rumbled out of the device. "You don't need to tell me. Ve didn't make it — right?"

"Right you are, Chief. We'll try again at five when we have the LSTs lashed on to both sides of us. If it doesn't work then, when the tide is low, we'll try again at high tide, in the early hours of the morning." A heavy sigh escaped his lips. "If you can keep up steam, so much the better, but do whatever's best for the engine."

"Vill do, Cap'n."

"Hey, since the patching job is done, could you send up any Oilers or Wipers you don't need down there? We could sure use some extra hands up here to help get the landing strips back aft. Earlier the Armed Guard were helping, but they went to their battle stations hours ago."

"Can do. They vill probably enjoy the opportunity to get out of this steaming hell hole, even if it does mean vork topside." The Chief began his coughing. "I'll send oop two Oilers, two Firemen, and two vipers right now. That's all I can spare."

Captain Daly waited again for the hacking to subside. "Send them to the number three hatch. Boats will fill them in on what their job will be if the Mate's not there." He wiggled his shoulders to relieve the tenseness. "Give your boys a hearty pat on the back for their extraordinary effort. They got us steam in record time under near impossible conditions. That goes for you, too, Chief! Thanks."

"Aye-aye, Cap'n."

Daly quickly stepped away from the communicator tube and slapped the brass handle of the mechanical device that signaled the engine room into the "Stop Engines" position. He scratched his head. Where in the devil could Cash be, he thought. He looked at his watch. Twenty or 30 minutes had elapsed since he'd called for the Mate. Although he no longer needed the helmsman, he did need an experienced person to talk to. Maybe, between the two of them, they could figure out something new . . . a different way to free the ship.

He leaned against the wheel. The let-down of the failed attempt, coupled with the long hours since they'd run aground, made his body feel like jelly. He'd been so sure that shifting all that weight to the stern would lift the bow enough to get the ship free. Head down, his hands on his hips, eyes closed, he let his mind play with different scenarios. There had to be a way. "Use your friggin' brain, Daly," he muttered under his breath. "Use your friggin brain!"

A moment later he strode the few steps to the doorway and stuck his head out. His voice carried down the companionway to the radio shack, some 15 feet away. "Hey, Sparks, come in here a minute!"

Chapter 8

JUNIOR, HEARING the Captain's voice, stuck his head around the corner and removed the earphones. "Sparks went down to the engine room to inspect the emergency batteries. They were due for their weekly hydrometer test. He thought they might be causing the communication problems. You want me to go get him?"

The Captain nodded. "Yeah. Wagner's back aft on the big gun with his men. I want to send a message and I need Sparks to help me code it."

Junior started down the companionway. "I'll get him, Sir."

Captain Daly walked into the chart room, still thinking through his new plan. Now he needed the Mate's cargo manifest. He poked into all the usual places, but couldn't find it. "Damn," he muttered.

"Where did Cash put it . . . and where in hell could he be? Why hasn't he reported to the bridge?" He stepped out onto the bridge wing, speaking trumpet in hand. Aiming it toward the bow, he said, "First Mate Cash, you're wanted on the bridge, immediately!" He pointed the horn toward the stern and repeated the message. This time he got results.

Within a minute he heard the Mate chugging up the ladder and pounding toward the bridge. He burst through the doorway, huffing and puffing.

"Where have you been?" the Captain asked. "I called for you half an hour ago."

"Down in the number three hold." Cash wheezed between words as he tried to fill his lungs with air. "The guys have done one hell of a job cleaning out those landing mats. They'll be finished before long." He took another big breath. "Were you looking for me?"

"I called for you when the Chief said we could put the ship in full astern. I was so damn sure we'd break free of the rocks, and I wanted you to get a helmsman up here. But that's not important now. What I need is for you to look at your cargo manifest and tell me what's in number one and number two holds. I couldn't find the damn thing. As I recall, it's a bunch of Jeeps."

"Give me a minute." Cash stepped into the chart room to get the clipboard that held the manifest. He had stashed it in back of the entertainment receiver. "Let's see now . . ." he stepped back into the wheel-house flipping pages. "Both holds carry Jeeps and their spare parts; they also have some odd-ball stuff like Jeep trailers. But mostly, they contain about ninety percent Jeeps, one-hundred-forty-eight to be exact. That seems to be about it." He looked up. "Anything else you need to know about the cargo?"

"That's all I need right now. You can go back to whatever you were doing, but keep your ears open. I may need you again real soon on a new project."

"Yes, Sir. I won't be down in the belly of the ship now. I'll be able to hear if you call."

As Cash walked out the door, Sparks sauntered in, his soft-topped, wooden clogs clunking on the deck. "You wanted to see me, Captain?" He tried to clear the salty sweat from his eyes, caused by his journey down to the engine room.

"I want to send a message, and I need you to work the code books with me." The Captain led the way into the chart room. "By the way, did the emergency batteries look OK? Are they the reason the system's down?"

Sparks shook his head. "They all checked good on the hydrometer test. Your problem is probably broken wires, not a short circuit."

Captain Daly wrinkled his nose. "Damn . . . Well, enough of that. We need to write down what has to be encoded. I'll dictate — you write."

Sparks cleared his eyes once more, then grabbed a piece of paper and a pencil from the high table. He scribbled the words as the Captain dictated.

> *The SS Albert A. Robinson is wedged tighter than earlier estimates. A full astern at high tide failed to release her. Doubtful the two LSTs can remove us from rocks. Request permission to jettison cargo in holds number one and two consisting of 148 Jeeps and spare parts. Less forward weight might raise the bow enough to free us from the rocks.*

"Sign it Captain Robert Daly."

Sparks jabbed a period on the paper as he finished writing, then held it out for the Old Man's approval.

Daly scanned the page. "Good, now let's get this sucker encoded." He stepped over to where the heavy, iron strong box sat, its four sides perforated with half-inch holes. They were put there to facilitate fast sinking in the event the ship were to fall into enemy hands. Heaved over the side into the briny water, the code books and all the ship's classified papers concerning destinations and convoy routes would find a quick and watery grave deep in the ocean. Lifting out the books, he instructed Sparks, "Get another piece of paper. I'll call out the code numbers — you write them down."

When the message had been coded, Sparks clomped his way to the radio shack to make the transmission.

No sooner had he left, than the Captain heard loud voices coming from the flying bridge. He scrambled up the ladder to see what caused all the commotion. Jumping off the last rung, he marched over to Wagner, who was peering through binoculars at the beach.

The gunnery officer spoke into his sound-powered phone system to the men in the ten gun tubs. His sharp words silenced the banter previously taking place among the gunners. "All right you guys, no more shootin' the bull. This is no longer Grandma's party line. I don't want to hear anything from anyone unless he sees something worth talking about. Look sharp. Be alert. Keep your eyes peeled up and down the beach. If you see some activity, I want to know." He drew in a breath. "They know we're here. You can be damn sure they aim to do something about it."

Daly frowned. "What's all the fuss about, Wagner?"

The gunnery officer lowered his field glasses. "The inevitable has finally happened, Captain. We spotted a Jap beach patrol about a thousand yards down the line."

Daly squinted in the direction Wagner indicated. "Where — I don't see anybody?"

"And you won't." Wagner raised his binoculars again and looked down the beach. "We swung the three-inch bow cannon in their direction and they took off into the underbrush. You can bet their eyes are on us right now, and they've already informed their headquarters we're here. I imagine it won't be too long before we find out what they intend to do about it."

Captain Daly pursed his lips. His palms turned damp. "I wonder how far their main base is from here. How long do you suppose it will take them to bring howitzers and troops through the jungle?"

Wagner hooked his teeth over his lower lip, a thoughtful expression creasing his face. "Not long for the troops, you can be sure of that. But, I suspect before they get here we'll get a visit from a reconnaissance plane. Good old Washing Machine Charlie will take a look and confirm our position." He dropped the field glasses and let them dangle from their strap, nestling next to his chest. He took a deep breath. "After that we may see some bombers."

Captain Daly swallowed the lump that rose in his throat. Earlier, he hadn't let himself fully believe they wouldn't get free of the rocks before being spotted. Now, he had to admit in all likelihood the ship would come under fire from a vastly superior force of men, at least in number, and all heavily armed. "It's your guess they'll be here before the LSTs get here at five o'clock?"

"There's not a doubt in my mind troops will come." Wagner shrugged, then raised his eyebrows. "But, the bright side is they might not be able to get heavy artillery here, like howitzers, before sundown, or maybe even tomorrow. We might have lucked out there where the heavy gear is concerned. Last night's tropical downpour will have muddied the heavy underbrush and jungle terrain, and turned it into one big swamp." Wagner crooked his index finger, motioning the Captain to follow him. "Let's go down to the chart room. I want to show you a map of Negros Island I found. I think you'll find it as interesting as I did."

Wagner slid down the ladder, two steps at a time, to the wheel-house, followed closely by Captain Daly. In a trot, they rounded the corner into the chart room. Wagner strode directly to a stack of individual island charts he'd discovered earlier when the Captain had been out on his inspection tour. He pulled one out. Spreading it across the large table top, he rubbed out the curl, placing a weight at one end. With his index finger he indicated an area of the map. "This is roughly where we are." He looked up. "Right?"

"Looks right to me."

"Here's the port of Bacolod where the airfield is. It looks to be about a hundred miles away from us." Beads of sweat dotted his forehead. He wiped them away with the back of his left hand. With a finger of his right hand he traced a heavy line. "This is the main road that comes down the east side of the island . . . down to the saw-tooth mountain range we can see off to our right. The road stops right here . . ." he jabbed at a spot on the map, "on the other side." He studied the serious expression on the Captain's face. "You get that? The road stops on the other side of the mountains."

Daly nodded. "Good." He flapped his shirt once or twice, billowing it out to make a cooling breeze.

Wagner dragged his finger down another heavy line running from Bacolod down the west side of the island. "This is the other major road. It too stops before crossing those craggy mountains we see to the north of us." Again he looked at the Captain. "As I see it, we're apparently sitting in a heavily overgrown area of Negros. It only represents about ten percent of the island's total mass, but it's rather inaccessible to heavy equipment like tanks and trucks. The paved roads don't come to this part of the island."

"I see what you're saying, but where did the beach patrol come from?" He flapped his shirt again. "Man, it's getting hotter."

Wagner rubbed the moisture from his brow. "No doubt they have a substantial garrison at this end of the mountain range. Their major responsibility would be to patrol. I'd assume their headquarters would be way over here where the deep-water dock is indicated. It's probably that group of soldiers that'll show up intending to annihilate us."

Looking intently at the Captain he raised his hand, his forefinger extended. "As I mentioned topside . . . from what this map shows, they'll have to come through some pretty dense undergrowth to get here. With the recent heavy rains, it's got to be a muddy swamp out there." He licked his dry lips. "It's my guess they'll not be able to bring any heavy-duty weapons with them." He leaned back against the bulkhead, shrugging his shoulders and raising his eyebrows. "At least not for a number of hours."

Captain Daly took one deep breath, exhaling slowly. "Man, that's good news — if any of this mess could be called good." He took another big breath and lifted his left hand. "With no big cannons to fear," he pushed down his first finger, "we can't be hurt by rifle fire —" another finger went down, "and they're not likely to try to storm us — not across two hundred yards of open water." A third finger curled over his palm, "What do we have to fear other than an air attack?"

"That's bad enough. Let's hope no 'Divine Wind' shows up."

"Divine Wind? What the hell is a Divine Wind?"

"That's what Kamikaze means. It comes from a time in Japanese history when, in the thirteenth century, a typhoon destroyed an invading army of Mongols."

"I didn't know where the term came from, but I do know what a Kamikaze is. And we sure don't want to see one of those. Barring that, what else should we be prepared for?"

Wagner shook his head. "Unfortunately, plenty." His lips formed a thin line as he drew them tightly together. "We can be pretty sure they'll be here fairly soon with portable mortars. In fact, I'd say you could bet your last dollar . . . and that can mean lots of trouble."

Captain Daly frowned. "Then, my next question is . . . do you have a plan of defense against a mortar barrage?"

The gunnery officer closed his eyes for a brief moment and rubbed his back against the door frame. "I have an idea I've been mulling around in my head all morning. I think it'll work." He held up his hand before the Captain, looking anxious, could speak. "Can I use the bridge for a meeting with my gunners? I'd like you to sit in on it, maybe even kibitz. It'll save time and keep me from having to repeat the plan."

Daly leaned back against the bulkhead wall. "Sure, sounds good to me."

"Let's go right now." Lieutenant Wagner grabbed a clipboard that had been laying on the table, marched into the wheel-house and plugged in his phone jack to one of the spotter station receptacles. "Now hear this! Listen up everyone! Starting at number one gun tub, check in with me. I want to know you're all up on the line."

One at a time the men in the eight 20mm antiaircraft gun tubs and the two 3-inch/50 guns sounded off. Wagner smiled. The boys sounded alert and ready. "OK, guys. I want to see one gunner from each emplacement in the wheel-house, on the double." He paused, thinking. "I also want the gunner who's left behind strapped into the harness of each of the twenty millimeters, just in case we get a surprise visit from the Nip air force. That's it. Let's move!" Holding up the board in his hand, he turned to the Captain. "Now I've got to make some quick notations and drawings on this clipboard before my men get here."

Wagner's pencil flew over the paper, making a rough sketch of the beach, the ship, the area between, and the probable placement of mortars. Within four minutes a representative from each of the guns arrived at the wheel-house, just as Wagner finished his drawing. With Captain Daly at his side, he faced the men. "Guys, we've got ourselves a problem here that none of us has been trained or prepared for. Our big guns, fore and aft, are designed for surfaced submarine and torpedo boat-type attacks for the most part." He held up his hand before anyone could argue. "Air attacks, too, I know, but because we have no range finders, the guns require fuses to be set, and the hand cranks are so slow that the twenty millimeters are our best antiaircraft weapon. That's specifically what they were designed for."

Wagner paused, briefly chewing the corner of his lip before continuing. "We're going to change all that right now, and here's the reason. In my opinion, and that of the Captain, there's no doubt we'll soon be attacked by ground forces . . . who, in all probability, will use mortars as their chief weapon. That means our twenty millimeters will be firing at fixed targets, not fast-moving aircraft like what you've been trained for. This gave me an idea I think will work. It sure as hell isn't in one of our Navy textbooks, but it's the best thing I could come up with."

He scanned the clipboard he held, made a couple more marks on it, then looked up, surveying the group of young men around him. "Here's the way we're going to knock out the ground forces' biggest threat . . . their mortars!"

He turned the board so all ten gunners could see his sketch. Using his pencil as a marker, he described the drawing he'd made.

"This is an aerial view, which shows the *Albert A. Robinson* in its present position on the rocks. About two hundred yards of water separate us from the sandy beach." He indicated each area as he spoke. "The beach extends back about thirty to forty yards, all sand. Beyond that is jungle. The enemy will probably come through the jungle to within ten or twenty yards of the sand. I assume that's where they'll set up their mortar launchers."

He looked around the room. "You with me so far?"

Every man in the wheel-house nodded.

Wagner continued. "Because of the distance of the sand and water, they'll have to be making mortar lobs of about two hundred-forty to two hundred-sixty yards. They'll need more than one shot to zero in on us from that distance. My plan is to disrupt their second shot. I'll tell you how in a minute, but before I get into it I want you all to understand another hidden danger. Sniper fire!"

He stopped, took a deep breath, and made eye contact with each of his men to make sure he had 100 percent of their attention before he continued. Their wide-eyed expressions told him he did.

"This is important! The snipers use extra long-barrel, twenty-five caliber carbines. Both the men and the guns are extremely accurate, so don't expose any part of your body for very long. If you do, we'll have a casualty on our hands. They also use a smokeless gunpowder. I think it's called Cordite. You'll see little or no smoke from their firing rifles. They learned the effectiveness of that in New Guinea. The snipers hid in coconut trees and picked off our officers, but were comparatively safe from returning fire because no tell-tale smoke could be seen to indicate where they were."

Wagner took a deep breath and continued. "Anyway . . . gunners strapped into the harnesses of the twenty-millimeters, and the loaders, should hunker their bodies low in the gun tub. You'll need to get low enough so you can just see the top half of the trees. That way you'll still be able to see the puff of smoke that'll tell you where the mortar fire originates, but your head will not be a target for their snipers."

Wagner paused. "Speaking of heads, you should all be wearing life jackets and helmets. Palmer . . . I notice you have no jacket on. I know they're hot as hell in the sun, but you will wear both of them. Is that understood?" Once again he caught the eye and received a nod of agreement from each man. He took another deep breath, releasing it like a slow leak.

"OK, here's the routine. Gunners and loaders will watch the beach area. Once you see the puff of smoke from the mortar, you'll stand and fire ten to twelve rounds into that location, then hunker down again before their marksmen can draw a bead on you. That's very important! Don't expose yourself any longer than you have to."

Captain Daly stood off to the side, his head nodding in agreement. Wagner could see the approval of his plan on the Captain's face. It gave him confidence the plan might work. He returned to his description of what he saw happening, if things went according to plan.

"Wham, wham, wham . . ." he waved his hands in an arc to show the trajectory of the fired ammo. "With the exploding heads of our twenty millimeters, and three or four of you firing, it's logical to assume we'll cause plenty of casualties. If nothing else, we'll make them scramble with their mortar launchers to a new location. They'll have to start all over again to get our correct range coordinates. That's what we want to do! Keep them scrambling with their mortars! They can't do us much damage if they can't zero in on us."

In the tropical heat, his enthusiasm and excited description caused sweat to bead on his forehead and drip from the tip of his nose. He impatiently wiped it away. "There's one thing you have to remember. Don't fire if there's ship's rigging or booms you might accidentally hit." He looked around the room again. "Do you have any questions?"

One gunner raised his hand.

Wagner nodded for him to go ahead.

"Do we have enough ammunition to handle this and an air attack, too?"

"Good question." Wagner frowned.

Just then Cash strolled in. "Oops, am I interrupting a meeting?"

"You're just the man I want to talk to." Wagner halfway smiled. "Do we have any twenty millimeter ammo in that mess of munitions in number five hold?" He hesitated when he saw the confusion on Cash's face. "If we do, can we get down to it with all those metal strips stacked all over it?"

Cash started toward the chart room. "I'll check the manifest."

"Let's hope," Wagner said to the Mate's back as Cash stepped through the doorway. He returned his attention to his crew of gunners. "The three-inch/fifty gun back aft will probably not be able to fire on the beach. It could possibly hit some of the ship's rigging, or the midship housing. But we might be able to use it if the mortar fire is thirty degrees or more off the bow to the left or right. Williams, you'll know when you get back to your station."

He briefly pursed his lips. "The three-inch cannon on the bow . . . well, that's a different story. I want you to set the barrel in a fixed, elevated position, aimed at the base of the trees; the ones set back about twenty or thirty feet from the beach. Once set, that elevation crank won't move while we fire at mortar emplacements. That keeps one man from being exposed to sniper fire."

He twisted his head back and forth to relieve the tension in his neck. "The man on the crank that moves the gun rotation from side to side . . . I think that's you, Palmer . . . will keep his eyes peeled for the mortar's puff of smoke, zero in on it as fast as possible, and take a single shot." He pointed at Palmer. "You'll call when to fire. The twenty millimeters will probably already be finished firing, giving you a good target of smoke and flying debris to zero in on. Fire your cannon into the mess of flames and smoke the twenties created, then reload and wait for the next mortar target to pulverize." He rubbed his palms together, visualizing the destruction of the enemy firing capabilities. "Any questions?"

Williams, from the aft 3-inch/50, raised his hand. "Do we have that many three-incher shells?"

Wagner squinted his eyes as he thought about it. "Maybe not. Let's cut down to every third or fourth mortar team we go after. They'll still scramble, thinking the 3-50 shell will be coming."

Gunner Palmer haltingly posed one. "Lieutenant, there's no protection from sniper fire from the side opposite the one where I might be firing."

Palmer's words were not clear to Wagner. "Explain."

"If I'm aimed twenty-five degrees off the starboard bow, a sniper twenty-five degrees off the port bow has a clear shot at me. Strapped in the saddle on the forward three-incher, I might just as well put a target on my back." He grinned. "You got any iron-clad shirt and pants I could wear?"

The whole group laughed.

Chapter 9

CAPTAIN DALY, who had been silent through the whole meeting, stepped forward. "I have an idea, Lieutenant Wagner."

"Get a bunch of large C clamps from the engine room . . . if they have any left . . . then take a group of those airstrip sheets and clamp them in front of the gunner on the steel protective shields already mounted on the three-inch gun. After they're firmly in place, bend them at a right angle. That should wrap around Palmer a hundred and eighty degrees. Those strips are thick enough to stop any Jap twenty-five bullet."

Wagner chewed his lip as he thought the suggestion through. "It's worth a try. I sure don't want anyone in a stationary position exposed."

"First things first." Captain Daly marched over to the tube that communicated with the engine room and blew hard into it. He waited for an answer, as did everyone else in the room.

"Yeah, bridge, this is the Third Engineer. Whatta ya want?"

"Captain Daly speaking. Do you have any C clamps left after making all your repairs?"

"Yes, Sir." Gallagher spoke hesitantly. "At least I think we do."

"Good. Gather up whatever you have. The bigger ones are better for what we plan to do. We'll need about a dozen. An Armed Guard man will be down shortly to pick then up."

"You got 'em, Captain. I'll get on it right away."

The talking tube snapped shut at both ends.

The Captain smiled as he turned back to Wagner. "They should be ready for pickup in a few minutes."

Wagner nodded, giving the Captain an "OK," with his thumb and forefinger together in a circle, then turned his attention back to his crew. "Palmer, when the meeting is over you head for the engine room and get those clamps.

"Now, are there any further questions on how we're going to disrupt those mortar teams?" A roomful of shaking heads answered his question. His men had a clear understanding of the battle plan he had put before them.

"OK, let's deal now with our biggest threat. It will still be from the air, and that's where the three-inch/fifty on the stern will be used. We're apt to be attacked by Zeros or bombers, or both, and all our training will be put to use." He turned to the Coxswain Third Class who was second in command and assigned to the rear big gun. "Williams, I know the three-incher has been proven rather ineffective against the fast little Jap Zeros. It's impossible to keep up with them with our manual hand cranks, and still get the proximity fuse settings to burst close to the target. So here's what we're going to do."

He paused to make sure Williams was intent on the words.

"The ammo for the three-incher comes two to a box. I want you to bring up several boxes and remove the covers. Pre-set one fuse in each box at three-thousand yards. That's the shell you'll fire first. The second one set for fifteen-hundred yards. You're working the vertical elevation crank and calling the fire, aren't you?"

Williams nodded "Yes, Sir."

"Here's the plan. When the approaching target is at about thirty-two hundred yards, let your first one go. Start cranking like a madman ahead of his flight path to let the second shell go within ten seconds of the first. The fuse settings may be off by a few hundred yards or so, but I want the pilot in that plane to think we have sophisticated, fast-firing antiaircraft guns on board. With these old guns that have no range finders we know that's wrong, but if we mechanically preset the fuses, we can get off two rapid shots. That might make him think we have an MK-37 fire-control system, like the ones the Navy destroyers carry. It might encourage him to drop his bombs from a much higher altitude. That's safer for him . . . and for us. Any questions?"

"Yes, Sir. What about snipers?"

"Good. You're thinking. You asked the question before I could get to it." He looked at the Captain. "How long would it take for Chips to fabricate a framing of about twenty-feet wide of two-by-fours across the front of the aft big gun tub? Our guys would help if he needed some grunts to schlep wood or anything else." He wiped the sweat from his forehead again. "What I have in mind is something that would allow us to lean a bunch of those airstrip plates on end against it. That would shield the aft three-fifty gunners and loaders from sniper fire from the beach."

"I'll get him on it. It should be relatively simple." Captain Daly turned to the gunner. "I'll have him report to you, Williams. You can supply him with the manpower he'll need to bring up framing material."

Palmer, the forward gunner, raised his hand.

Wagner nodded for him to go ahead.

"Suppose the Jap planes are coming in from the bow? Or, for that matter, they enter our target area from the stern and exit over the bow, do I ignore them?"

"You're right. That could definitely happen." Lieutenant Wagner squinted his eyes in thought. "No, you won't ignore them. Have two cases of shells on your deck with the fuses set the same as the aft gun. Your vertical gunner will have to do the same fast-cranking as Williams. If there are enough of those C clamps you're picking up, maybe you can give some protection to the vertical cranker, too."

Palmer nodded. "Leave it to us. We'll dummy-up something, Lieutenant."

Ivan climbed the outside ladder to the wheel-house and walked in on the gathered group. "I hope I'm not interrupting anything."

Captain Daly shook his head. "It's OK, but make it short."

"I just wanted to let you know the crew and I have all but cleaned out number three hold. We have steel sheets everywhere you can imagine back aft. The stack on top of number five hold is seven feet high, as well as all around it. Even the fan-tail is covered." He grinned. With an exaggerated motion he wiped his brow. "The guys have done a Herculean job! They're stacking the last of the strips alongside number four hold just to get all the weight possible out of number three. They'll be finished in a few minutes, and I'm going to knock them off for a well-deserved rest. Is that OK?"

The Mate, returning from the chart room, had caught Ivan's report. "Hey, good job, man . . . but stick around for a minute. I've got another job for you."

The Third Mate's shoulders visibly drooped. Anybody could see he'd about run out of gas. Even so, he didn't complain.

Cash, the clipboard with the manifest in his hand, turned his attention to Wagner. "We're in luck. We've got enough twenty millimeter ammo on the 'tween deck to start a revolution. Whether we can get to it or not is a whole different question, but it's down there somewhere." His gaze returned to Ivan. "I want you to grab four or five of your guys and look for this ammo." Cash shrugged his shoulders as if to say, "I'm sorry, but it can't be helped." He looked at Ivan. "I know you and your crew are pooped. It's understandable. You've just accomplished an almost impossible job, but we need that ammo, and we need it now."

Ivan dripped sweat from every pore. His shirt, as wet as if he'd just pulled it from the wash basin, clung to his body. He rubbed a weary hand across his eyes. His head hung to the side, exhaustion apparent in every line of his body. The heat and heavy exertion of the last nine hours had taken its toll. "How do you propose we get down in number five?" He looked up at Cash from under tired eyelids. "We've covered all entrances on the mast house and aft housing. Don't tell me we have to remove the plates we just got finished stacking."

Cash started to chuckle. "No, no, no. There's a much simpler way. You'll go down the air scoops."

Ivan's head jerked up. "What?"

"You can use the air scoops. They're three feet in diameter. You'll have no trouble fitting. They have ladder bars welded on the inside. All you have to do is unscrew and remove the screening over the vent openings. That's no problem."

"No problem? They're probably held solid with paint."

"If there's too much paint on the screw heads, and there probably is, use a cold chisel and hammer to knock the heads off." He went through the motions of the technique he'd just suggested. "After you get those suckers off, pull the wire screen towards you, and shove it out of the way. Then . . . down you go."

Even Ivan's smile looked tired. "That sounds easy enough. It sure beats moving those plates again!" He sighed slowly and deeply. "I guess we can do that." He turned to go.

Captain Daly stopped him. "Be sure to take four or five strong guys with you. You'll need them. And make sure everyone has a flashlight." He paused. "Also, you might remind them they're moving ammo, not cotton bales."

Ivan had to smile at that. "I'll do that, Sir, and get back to you as soon as I can, probably within the hour. I hope we don't run into a problem. We won't be able to look at any crates below the top two layers. There's just too much weight involved, even for our strongest muscle men. But, if what we're looking for is on the upper part of the 'tween deck cargo, we'll find it." Once again he turned to leave.

Captain Daly patted his shoulder. "I know you and your guys are exhausted. Give them another pat on the back from me. Oh, by the way, was Chips hauling steel for you?"

"Yes, Sir."

"Tell him to come to the bridge. We have a special project for him."

Ivan nodded. "Will do." He looked at Cash and Wagner. "If there's nothing else, I'll get busy on this treasure hunt." He halfway raised his hand in a wave as he walked out.

Captain Daly looked at Lieutenant Wagner. "This way Williams can wait here for Chips. It'll give you time to explain what you had in mind for the protective framing to hold the metal sheets."

Wagner nodded in approval. Snapping his fingers he grabbed everyone's attention. "OK, men. We've made our game plan. Now you have to go back to your guns and bring the other guys up to speed. Explain to them how we're going to prevent the Japs from zeroing in on us with their mortars. Once you're sure they understand, make lots of make-believe dry runs. Go through what each man is supposed to do when those puffs from a mortar team are sighted. No live ammunition, of course, but go through a lot of imagined attacks. When the real thing happens, we want everyone to know their procedures and responsibilities. Now get back to your tubs and start teaching."

The men turned to go.

"Just a minute." The Lieutenant held up his hand for them to pause. "Don't forget, while your team is learning its duties, all of you still have to keep your eyes peeled on the jungle as well as up and down the beach. If anyone sees anything unusual, sound off loud and clear. Yell it out so we all can hear! And be sure you caution the merchant seamen who volunteered on the twenties about all we discussed . . . especially regarding snipers and how to avoid getting picked off." He swiveled his head while he took in then exhaled a deep breath. "I guess that's all. Get goin'."

He pointed at Williams. "All but you, of course. When Chips gets here I want the two of you to get that shield up as fast as possible. Use your men on the aft three-incher to help him. If you need more grunts, grab them from the number eight and nine tubs. I'm sure Chips will tell you how much material he'll need and where to get it."

All heads turned toward the doorway when they heard the sound of Sparks clogs clomping down the companionway. He rounded the corner, entering the wheel-house with a message in his hand, and stopped short. Surprise radiated from his eyes. "Excuse me, Captain, I didn't mean to interrupt, but here's the answer to your question about the cargo in number one and two hold. Will you need me to help decode it?"

Captain Daly cocked his head to one side, his eyebrows arched in question, and looked at Wagner. "Busy?"

"Not as long as the message's a short one." He pulled the plug on his phone system as he talked, then turned to Williams. "I guess you and Chips can come up with ideas for the necessary shielding without me. As soon as he gets here, you two had better take off and get started on the job."

The tall, shy Ship's Carpenter slouched into the room. "D-d-did you want to s-see me, C-c-captain?"

"Lieutenant Wagner needs your talent. He'll explain what he wants."

He faced Wagner. "What c-c-can I d-do for you?"

Wagner pointed at his gunner. "You know Williams?"

Chips nodded.

"I want the two of you to design a sniper shield for the aft three-incher. I'm needed here to help the Captain decode a message, but this is urgent, Chips. I stress the word urgent. Williams will explain where it's to be built and what it's to accomplish. You can take it from there. Show us how the shield should be constructed . . . and do it as quickly as you can."

Again Chips nodded. He seldom spoke unless he had to. He and Williams headed out the starboard wing.

Sparks stood waiting.

Captain Daly grinned. "Thanks for bringing the message. I don't need you to help me this time. Wagner and I can handle this one."

"Yes, Sir." Sparks clomped out of the room.

Wagner and Daly entered the chart room, followed by the Mate. The two code books had been shoved to the corner of the table. Wagner dragged them forward and shoved one over to the Captain. Together they worked on transposing the five-number code groups into words. When they finally finished, they spread the message on the table so that the Mate could see it, too.

> *Jeeps should not be jettisoned unless there is no other way to free your vessel. Pacific Command.*

Captain Daly knew he had a smirk on his face. He smacked his open hand with a closed fist. "Hot damn! They didn't tell me I couldn't. I intend to get off this damn rock pile on the next try, so over the side they go." He caught the Mate's eye.

"Cash, get some boys up forward and start removing the hatch covers. Also start rigging the booms for work on both number one and number two. You'd better get Boats out to man the winches." He frowned, his brows making a line across his forehead as he tried to think of all that needed doing. "While you're at it, you might just as well have the guys remove the strong backs and tarps from both hatches. Have them leave the boards on number two for the time being, at least until we see if we can dump the Jeeps from number one."

Cash wiped the perspiration from his forehead with the back of his hand. "Captain, got any slick ideas how we're going to release the Jeeps once they're over the side?"

The Captain squinted his eyes as he scanned the ceiling in thought.

"Yeah. We'll use the four-chain rig the Army boys used to load the fifty-five gallon drums of diesel fuel aboard. That should work."

Cash mused out loud. "Those hooks on the end of the chains did hold tight until slack was given once they were down in the hold."

"You got it."

The Mate grinned. "We'll have to find a place to put those four metal hooks so when Boats drops the Jeep into the water, the momentary flotation lets the headache weight ball hit the Jeep. That ought to allow the necessary slack in the chains to release the hooks. That shouldn't be too hard to figure out."

Captain Daly billowed his sweat-soaked khaki shirt. "I'm sure the Army guys left that nifty little rig to help us unload once we get to Lingayan. It's probably in the Boatswain's locker. When you catch up with Boats, have him drag it out."

"Will do, Captain." Cash hesitated.

"Get going. I'll call the engine room and get steam for the winches."

Cash took off in a hurry to do as the Captain had ordered.

Captain Daly walked the few steps to the engine room communicator tube and blew into it as hard as he could.

"Yeesus *Christ*, vot is it dis time?" The Chief finished the sentence with his usual smoker's hack.

The Captain waited for the coughing to subside. "I need steam now on the winches for number one and two holds. OK? Can you do that?"

"Aye. No problem." He cleared his throat. "Have you seen any Japs yet, Cap'n?"

"No, and I hope I won't. In fact, if I never see another one in my entire lifetime, it will be just fine with me."

The Chief laughed as he coughed. "Steam comin' oop, Cap'n."

The tube snapped closed at both ends.

Men scurried to complete their assignments. They rigged the booms, removed the hatch covers, and prepared to help unload the designated holds. Soon, the *chug-chug-chug* of the winches echoed throughout the ship, as Boats removed the hatch beams and got started on hold number one. One after the other he unceremoniously pulled up a Jeep and dropped it over the side. Bubbles rose around each one as it settled to the bottom.

Captain Daly, Wagner, and Cash watched the performance from the bridge. Cash grinned. "I got dibbs on salvaging those little darlings after the war."

The humor in the remark tickled the Captain. He decided to play along. "I'll match you for it. Heads or tails?" he pulled a nickel from his pocket and flipped it in the air.

The coin hadn't returned to his hand when a shout came out of gun tub number two. "We've got visitors twenty degrees off the starboard bow!"

Wagner scrambled up the ladder to the flying bridge next to gun tub number four. Hurriedly he plugged his phone line into the jack so he could talk to all the gun emplacements. "Hunker down, men. Watch yourselves!"

He took his instructions to heart. Tightening the chin strap of his helmet, he lowered himself behind the gun tub, allowing only enough of himself to show so he could see. He discerned movements of a curious nature in the trees lining the sand. Whoever they are, he thought, they're not trying to keep their presence a secret, but they're not exposing themselves either.

He spoke into the phone. "Hold your fire, men." The speaking trumpet lay on the deck where it had been left. He snatched it up and handed it into the gun tub. "Martinez, take this loud hailer and ask them in Spanish if they're Filipino."

"Yes, Sir." The gunner stood and took the horn. "Attention on shore." The Spanish rolled off his tongue. "If you are Filipinos you are instructed to leave the area immediately," he paused for a split-second, "or you will be shot!" He waited three seconds then repeated the message one more time. He leaned over the rim of the tub and turned his head to tell Wagner what had been said.

They both heard the whine of the bullet as it whizzed past Martinez's ear. A split-second later they heard the crack of the rifle that had been fired. Everyone, the gunners in the tub and Wagner next to it, hit the deck.

"Look sharp, guys. We're being fired upon." Wagner spoke into the phone from his prone position.

"Hey, Lieutenant. Here's the horn." Martinez handed it over the edge of the tub, exposing only his arm to do so. "I'm sure glad I turned my head when I did. I'll have to say, I don't think they're Filipinos."

Chapter 10

WHEN THE ENEMY had been spotted, most of the men had provided themselves with some sort of protection. They'd taken at least minimal precautions. The crack of the rifle had driven them all under cover . . . all but Boats, the Bosun. The noisy winches had drowned out the early warning yelled by a crew member, as well as the sound of the rifle shot.

When Lieutenant Wagner saw another Jeep come up from the hold, he realized what had happened. Boats would definitely be a target if he didn't take immediate cover.

Wagner yelled at him into the speaking trumpet. When there was no response, he called again.

The winches continued to chug.

Wagner knew his message hadn't been heard. He yelled into the

phones that connected him to the gun tubs. "Someone up there tell Boats to take cover. You guys in tubs one and two, throw a shoe or something at him if necessary, but get his attention!"

Moments later the winches no longer chugged. Boats had gotten the message.

Captain Daly yelled up to the flying bridge. "As long as you have the trumpet and the winches are quiet, tell Boats I want him in the wheel-house ASAP. Instruct him to hug the outside rail and crawl on all fours, so he won't be a target."

Lieutenant Wagner quickly relayed the Captain's orders.

Captain Daly thought about the man he'd ordered to the bridge. Many Bosuns were given the handle of "Boats," but none were as unusual and colorful as the man on the *Albert A.* During his career as a maritime sailor, he had indulged in covering his now flabby, 50-year-old body with tattoos — so many, that not even two square inches of unadorned skin could be found anywhere on his person, from the neck down. On top of that, he rarely wore a shirt. Splotches of red lead paint, as well as warship gray, decorated his exposed skin, from his ankles to the top of his bald head. His khaki cutoffs, unwashed for the duration of the trip and saturated with paint, no doubt could stand up in the corner by themselves.

The Captain smiled to himself as he pictured the man.

If anyone were foolish enough to ask Boats just how much of his body under those stiff cutoffs had tattoos, he'd gladly offer to unzip to show them. He'd even volunteer to tell a side-splitting story of how the tattooed dots and quarter-inch dashes on his manhood would turn to images of gargoyles, crocodiles, ugly snakes, or worse when he became sexually aroused. A colorful character if there ever was one, Boats was nevertheless a welcome addition to the Captain's crew.

Daly's head jerked up, torn from his thoughts of the last few minutes, when Boats entered the room.

"Captain, Sir . . . did you want to see me?"

"Yes, Boats, I did. I'm glad you got started on hold number one. How far did you get?"

Hitching up his beltless cutoffs, which usually hung low on his hips, he cleared his throat. "Probably a little more than twenty percent. You want me to go finish the job?"

The Captain frowned as he brushed his hand across his short hair in what was becoming a predictable nervous response. "Well . . . yes . . . but not without protection." He leaned back against the bulkhead. "I've got a question for you. Can you operate the winches when you're sitting on your butt?"

Boats acknowledged he could. "But I can work only one at a time that way." He pantomimed the up-and-down motion required with his hands clasped over his head. "The way I have it rigged right now, one man can work both winches." He put his arms at his sides and pumped them up and down, then pulled up his drooping cutoffs again.

Cash, who had entered the wheel-house seconds after Boats, broke into the conversation. "Two people could handle both winches sitting on their butts if they worked as a team . . . right?"

Boats rubbed his bearded chin. "Sure . . . it could be done. But it'd be a little slower. We'd probably bump the edges of the hold opening a few times. We wouldn't be able to see the cargo coming up from below. The three-foot hatch riser would block our vision." He grinned. "I don't suppose a few dented hoods on those Jeeps would matter since we're dumping them anyway."

Cash smiled. "Captain, I've worked cargo winches before, up in the Aleutian Islands when I sailed on a reefer ship." He pointed between himself and Boats. "The two of us, sitting on our butts, would be protected from any small arms fire by the riser and winch engines. We'd be fine as long as we didn't stand up."

"You got it, Cash." Captain Daly pointed at the Mate. "That's exactly what I've been thinking." He turned to Boats. "Are the two seamen still waiting for you down in the hold?"

Boats nodded his shiny hairless head. "I've got three down there now because they have to push the Jeeps into position. I'm sure they're still down there —" he rubbed a trickle of sweat from his forehead, "at least they'd better be. I told 'em I'd be right back." He paused to blow his nose on an old paint rag. The red handkerchief, always rolled and tied around his neck, was never used for that purpose. It stayed tied in place, permanently — to ward off bad spirits and bring good luck he told everyone.

"OK, it sounds like you and Cash can handle the job. The two of you get back up there and see if you can finish emptying hold number one, but be careful. They've got sharpshooters over there that would like nothing better than to pick off one of you."

Lieutenant Wagner walked in and heard the last part of the conversation. "I have an idea that will cut down the possibility of sniper fire on you guys." He ran his tongue over his lips. "You'll probably be running up the starboard side of the ship. I'll have the four twenty millimeters on that side spray the tree line with about ten rounds each as you make your run for the winches. When those exploding head shells hit the beach, I have a hunch the Japs will all be ducking behind some coconut tree — at least they will if they have an ounce of sense. Be ready to start your dash in fifteen minutes. When you hear the guns begin to fire, you get your butts in gear and run to the winches."

Cash smiled. "That'll work." Boats agreed.

The Lieutenant slapped Cash on the shoulder. "Just get going. I'll issue instructions to my men right now."

Cash headed for the door, a wide grin on his face. "Hear, hear! Let's hear it for the Navy Armed Guard!" He and Boats took off in a trot down through the midship housing.

Captain Daly let a smile creep onto his face. "Good thinking, Wagner. I commend you." He cocked his head to one side, one eyebrow raised. "Now comes the big question."

"What's that, Captain?"

"How long will it be before those guys on the beach start lobbing in mortar shells?"

Wagner looked at his watch.

He looked at the ceiling.

He looked around the room.

His brow furrowed as he debated on the answer.

"Well, they did a good job to get here as fast as they did. They had to come through some pretty dense undergrowth.

"It could be their barracks are not that far from the village those kids came from. And mortar launchers are no doubt a part of the arsenal they arrived with. . . . They're probably setting them up right now." He looked again at his watch.

"It'd be my guess we could expect a few to come our way within the next half hour." His eyes caught the Captain's. "That's the way I see it."

Nodding, Captain Daly expelled the deep breath — almost a sigh — he had been holding back. "That sounds logical." He leaned back against the bulkhead, his arms folded across his chest. "What else does your crystal ball tell you?"

Lieutenant Wagner chuckled at the thought, then promptly sobered. "We can assume they have no intentions of storming us. I'm sure to them we're already a casualty; just a used-up pile of steel, stuck on their beach and unable to free ourselves. They know if we could get loose, we would have been long gone by now." He flexed his left hand, the one that had been holding his clipboard — almost a death grip. "I'm sure they feel time is on their side."

Captain Daly nodded slowly. "That makes sense, but they might feel differently when they see us resume dumping Jeeps over the side."

"You're right there, and for sure they'll change their ideas about us when they see those two LSTs come over the horizon." Wagner looked again at his watch. "The fifteen minutes is almost up. Time to test the plan. Let's see if Cash and Boats can make it safely to number one." He turned on his phone system again. "Listen up, guys! Guns two, four, and six, I want you to lay down a barrage for about ten seconds at the tree line. Commence firing in fifteen seconds."

The antiaircraft guns broke the silence, each shot from each gun about a half-second apart. The shells echoed back as they hit the beach and trees and exploded. Shell smoke lay in a cloud, obscuring the beach.

Seconds later, it was silent.

Not one round of fire had come from the enemy position during the barrage. Cash and Boats had made their dash to number one safely. Quickly, they put in action the method they'd devised and soon the chugging of the steam release and the grinding of the winch gears filled the air. Another Jeep rose precariously from the hold, swung over the side, and dropped into the water.

In the distance, the drone of a single-engine airplane could be heard. All eyes turned in the direction of the sound. Someone in tub number three yelled, "There it is — coming in over the bow at two o'clock!"

All work came to a screeching halt. The merchant seamen scrambled for cover or headed for the midship housing.

Lieutenant Wagner, with the Captain at his side, found the plane through his binoculars. "It's Japanese."

Activating his phone, he spoke to his men. "This plane knows exactly what he's looking for. Obviously, his mission is to destroy the Liberty ship floundering on the shore of their island . . . that's us, men. Look sharp!"

The plane circled in from the southwest where the sun was in a direct line with his approach. It began to descend toward the stern of the ship.

Standing on the flying bridge, Wagner surveyed the situation and gave directions to his men. "It's a Zero fighter — carrier type. He could have two good-sized bombs. You guys on the twenties, hold your fire until he's down low enough to get a hit. Williams, you can fire the three-incher per our plan."

The Japanese pilot leveled off some 2,000 yards up, to make his first bombing run.

The aft big gun belched out its first shell with a deafening roar. The pre-set blast exploded well behind the speedy Zero.

The 20mms commenced barking their defiance at the plane's presence.

The aft three-incher sent its second fused shell ten seconds later, with almost identical results as the first. Not close, but fast enough, hopefully, to make the pilot think the ship might have an MK-37 fire control range finder.

Like a cluster of shooting stars on a clear night, tracers flooded the sky in the vicinity of the fast-approaching plane. Wagner watched closely as it passed overhead. When he saw the first bomb released, he yelled to his men, "Hit the deck!" — then jumped into gun tub number four.

Fortunately, the pilot had released the bomb at too high an altitude to provide any accuracy. It fell a good 50 yards off the stern of the ship.

The Lieutenant made an attempt to calm his young crew. "I know you're understandably shaken up, guys. Take several deep breaths to get your nerves under control. Remember your training — lead him, don't just put your sights on him and fire." He paused for a second or two. "OK, everything's under control. Let's get him when he makes another run."

Wagner watched the Zero sweep around. Since the gunners hadn't come close to him before, apparently the pilot felt a little braver. He started his run at a lower altitude, again approaching from the stern.

"He's taking a big gamble this time, men. I think he has it in his head to finish us off with his second bomb. Let's give him a little early warning this run. Maybe when he sees what he'll be flying into it will disrupt his accuracy. OK . . . guys . . . give him hell!"

Smoke and flames poured from the 20mm guns. The big three-incher got off the two pre-fused shots, the second a near miss. Wagner couldn't believe his eyes. Twenty millimeter tracers zipped in front of, behind, and on both sides of the speedy Zero, but no meaningful hits occurred. How can this be? he asked himself. How can that "Charlie" be so lucky? As the plane passed overhead, he saw the release of the second bomb.

"Hit the deck!" He yelled so loud he wouldn't have needed a phone system; his gunners could have heard him without it. All but three of the 20s stopped firing, the men hunkering down low in the gun tubs.

The bomb hit the water no more than 25 feet off the port side, just opposite the number five munitions hold. The *Albert A.* shuddered, back and forth. Men back aft who had been standing, but not holding on to anything, found themselves on their knees, or on their backsides. The force of the explosion threw water and mud 40 feet in the air, showering the men in gun tub number nine.

Wagner, still taking cover in tub number four, commended his gunners. "Good shooting, guys! He got the message on that run. The Zeros only carry two bombs. He's dropped those. He has two thirty-caliber machine guns and two twenty-millimeter cannons. He might be foolish enough to make a strafing run, so keep your eyes on him."

Suddenly, a burst of small arms fire broke loose from the beach area. The men standing in the gun tubs had their backs exposed to this unexpected fire as they watched the Zero. Quickly, they took cover, getting as low as they could in the tubs, and pointing their guns skyward.

Perry, the loader in gun tub six, no more than ten yards from Wagner on the midship housing, yelled, "Lieutenant . . . Summerfield got hit in the shoulder!"

Wagner cautiously stuck his head over the protective rim of number four, and yelled, "Hey, Summerfield . . . you hurt bad?"

"I'll live . . . but I can't use my left hand, Sir."

"Can you walk?"

"Yes, Sir."

"Perry, if your magazine isn't near full, dump it and put in a fresh cartridge. Summerfield, you get below to the officer's mess. Doc'll patch you up, but be careful going down."

Knowing Josh was in the wheel-house, Wagner yelled down to him. "Hey, Josh — get one of the gunnery volunteers up here fast to fill in for Summerfield in number six tub. We need him to feed ammo."

"I'm on my way."

Wagner turned in time to see Perry help Summerfield out of the gunner's harness. "Perry, you get strapped in. You're the new gunner. A merchant seaman, one of the volunteers, will be up shortly to be your loader. Make sure Summerfield leaves his helmet behind."

"Will do. You can be sure I'll welcome him with open arms when he gets here."

Suddenly the sound of a mortar came from somewhere in the jungle. The first shot went clear over the ship and landed 30 yards astern. "Did anyone see where that baby came from?" Wagner scanned the beach area but could see no sign of where the enemy hid.

"We were all watching the Jap plane, I guess." Martinez shook his head. "Not too smart."

Wagner nodded. He spoke into his phone system. "You guys better keep your eyes on the beach. I'll watch the Charlie." He paused to take another look at the plane. "It looks like he's heading for home. One of you guys might have nicked him and he feels the need for some repairs. Don't get too elated, though. You can be sure he'll tell his home base our location. That means we'll probably be seeing some of his friends real soon."

Another mortar thudded in from the beach area.

"There it is!" A gunner on the port side commenced firing at the tell-tale puff of smoke. Within two seconds the other three port-side 20s were pouring shells into the area. Six seconds later the 3-inch/50 cannon on the bow unloaded with a shot that shook the whole ship when it left the muzzle, and again when the shell exploded in the clearing area, some 250 yards away.

"All right!" Wagner threw his right arm up in a thumbs-up motion. "Man, you guys converted a chunk of jungle into a desert in less than twenty seconds. Nice shooting, but keep alert. There'll be more and more coming in soon."

The words were barely out of his mouth when another mortar thud sounded from the starboard side. Two tubs immediately answered the puff of smoke from the enemy launcher, a third and then a fourth joining in.

"Keep cleaning them up you guys so they can't adjust and zero in on their target. We've got to keep them moving." Wagner jumped out of the tub he'd been in and headed for the safer area on the starboard bridge wing, under the number four gun.

Two more mortar "*thunks*" sounded, originating no more than 30 feet apart. Guns blazed in four tubs, raking the positions of the launches. Exploding bullets sent up puffs of sand as they shattered everything in their path. Grass and trees smoldered in the target area. And then the *coup de grâcé*, the big gun put a shell right in the middle of the region covered by the other guns.

"Now you've got the system, guys . . . keep it up," Wagner shouted from his new strategically located position.

Another mortar shell hit the rear metal lifeboat on the port side, blowing it to bits. Chunks of wooden oars and seats, all on fire, littered the air. Pieces of oil soaked canvas added to the flaming debris, some of it landing in the lifeboat just in front of the one destroyed.

Captain Daly, seeing the damage from the port-side wing, quickly assessed the situation. He turned to his Second Mate, who had returned from getting a substitute loader. "Josh, don't expose yourself to sniper fire, but get someone up here with a fire hose to douse those burning pieces on that good life boat before it catches fire. We can't let it be destroyed, too."

Josh hurried to the seamen's mess hall. There he found Olson dipping into the BBB. "Drop the ladle, Olson, and come with me. I've got a short job for you."

The tall, skinny seaman questioned, "What?"

"I need you to douse some burning pieces of wood." He sent the man on his way, instructing him to put out the fire threatening the undamaged lifeboat from the back of the bridge deck, from where he would be safe from sniper fire. Josh headed back to the bridge.

Incoming mortar continued from the wooded area, along with small-arms rifle fire, as the Japs increased the frequency of their bombardment. The ship's 20s blazed away almost constantly, trying to force the mortar launching stations to move.

Just as Josh returned to the bridge, a mortar shell hit the number three hold cover. He hurried to the bridge wing, where Wagner stood, and looked down to see what damage may have occurred.

Several of the recently reassembled three-by-five hatch boards had splintered into fiery bits of wood and dropped down to start small fires on the wooden dunnage in the bottom of the now empty 'tween deck area of the number three hold. He knew he had better do something about that, and fast.

Josh shouted to the Captain. "Do we know if the steam-smothering fire system is working in the 'tween deck area? We've got a fire in the dunnage in number three."

The Captain shook his head. "You'd better take care of it with a fire hose. I'm sure it's not on the Chief's priority list. I don't want to pull any more of his men away from the engine room repairs. Besides, the fire hose will do the job much faster. I intend to get off these damn rocks when the LSTs arrive. Let's not bug the Chief with a problem the deck crew can handle."

Josh turned toward Wagner. "Lieutenant, in about three or four minutes can I get you to have your men lay down another one of those beach barrages? I've got to fight that fire down in the number three hold, and my boys will be exposed while they get some men and a hose below to put it out. Can you do that?"

"We'll do our best. Be ready in three minutes and I'll see that you have some cover fire." Wagner flipped on his phone switch and gave the instructions to his gunners . . . "But wait for my order to fire!"

Chapter 11

JOSH RACED to the door of the midship companionway, slid down the two ladders that led to the main deck, and sprinted back to the seamen's mess hall. He thought he should be able to recruit some seamen there. Skidding to a halt at the doorway, he looked around and smiled. Three men had just sat down to relax.

"Speier, Blake, Rork, I need you — *now*! There's a fire in the dunnage at the bottom of the 'tween deck of number three. We have to put it out before it burns through the hatch boards to the wood cargo in the lower deck."

Tired as they were, the three jumped up and followed Josh, briskly walking down the companionway as he explained what he wanted them to do.

"Rork, when we get outside, wait for my order, then make a dash for the mast-house entrance. Get to the 'tween deck and look for the fire hose that will be within your reach."

The seaman nodded his understanding.

"There's a fifty-foot hose right outside this door. You two," he pointed at Blake and Speier, "grab it when Rork goes, drag it to number three and lower it down far enough so Rork can reach it. Give him a little extra slack. Scooch down below the railing and wait. When you see the hose moving — Rork will give it a good tug to let you know he has a hold of it — you hustle back here and turn on the water for him. Then both of you get below and help him snuff out that fire. Understood?"

"Yes, Sir," all three said in unison.

Josh looked at his watch. "OK — get ready. When we hear a steady fire from the gunners we'll —"

The 20s commenced raking the beach area where the snipers appeared to be.

"That's it! Go! Go!"

Back in the chart room, Captain Daly had come to a decision. He yelled down the companionway, "Sparks, I need you, right now!"

The radio operator, glad to remove the uncomfortable earphones and turn the radio room over to Junior, hurried to answer the Captain's call.

"Sparks, I've been thinking. Since the Pacific Command seems to think our cargo is extremely important to the success of the invasion landing, I'm wondering if it wouldn't be worth our while to ask them for some air support. I don't know where it would come from, or even if they'd send it, but I don't think it'd hurt to ask. Who knows, there might even be a task force with some carriers in the area."

"Sounds good to me, and Lord knows, we could sure use a little help here."

"One problem, though. Lieutenant Wagner and I are too busy to code up the message at this time." The Captain rubbed his hand across his tired eyes. "Or, maybe we could send it out uncoded. What do you think?"

Sparks blinked his eyes a couple of times. "I suppose we could. I've logged uncoded messages from other ships in trouble. Who are we afraid might hear our message asking for help? The Japs already know we're in trouble." He grinned. "Anyway, who'd want to put a direction-finder fix on our location that doesn't already know we're here?"

"Good point, Sparks. Just send the message. Tell them we're under fire from land and air. Use that new frequency Pacific Command gave you . . . and don't mention our cargo or where we're heading, just that we want — no — need air support!"

"You got it, Captain, and it's going out *uncoded* . . . right?"

"That's right — now get that baby on the air, ASAP." Smiling, Daly pointed his index finger at the door.

Sparks strode back to the radio shack, fired up the transmitter, and broke radio silence with an uncoded message to the Pacific Command, the first time he'd done that in his 16 months as a radio operator. His hand anxiously keyed the dots and dashes.

> *WE ARE UNDER AIR ATTACK AND GROUND MORTAR FIRE. NEED AIR SUPPORT WITH STRAFING ABILITIES IMMEDIATELY.*
>
> *CAPTAIN ROBERT DALY*
> *ALBERT A ROBINSON*

Sparks received an immediate reply, also uncoded.

WE HAVE YOUR MESSAGE. The standard closing letters *AR VA* followed the brief response, signifying "end of message" and "end of transmission."

Sparks finished recording the curt note and handed it to Junior. "Take this to Captain Daly. Tell him I sent the message, and this is the answer I got."

Junior limped to the chart room and handed the slip of paper to the Captain.

"Good," he said, "and thanks, Junior." He gently slapped him on the back. "Maybe we'll get some help."

The *thunk* of launched mortar shells seemed almost rhythmic in their timing, as they continued to explode around the ship. One hit directly on the pile of iron sheets covering hold number five. Every metal hauler who witnessed the flying pieces of metal knew that it had saved their lives. All their sweat, blisters, and aching muscles had been well worth the nine-hour marathon they'd raced to complete. Had they not accomplished that task, they'd surely be shark "chum" right now.

For certain, all the deck officers knew that had it not been for Josh's idea, in all probability their war, their dreams for the future, their very lives would have been over.

Five minutes after the hit, Ivan emerged from the air scoop alongside the number five hold, his five men close behind him. They paused a second or two to let their eyes adapt to the bright sunlight, then dropped down, one at a time, to the metal sheets and then to the deck. In a line, they all scurried crab-style to the entrance to the midship housing. Ivan headed for the bridge; the five seamen went off in the direction of the crew mess to await further orders.

Ivan stepped into the wheel-house and on out to the bridge wing to find the gunnery officer in his usual spot. "Hey, Lieutenant, we found the twenty millimeter ammo in the 'tween deck munitions hold. We'd just located it when that mortar round hit the metal plates over our heads. What a noise!" He clamped his hands over his ears, clenched his teeth, and shut his eyes for effect. "Kee-*rash*! We all thought we were about to meet our Maker. My ears are still ringing!"

Wagner smiled. "I guess it would have been pretty loud where you were, enclosed like that."

"Anyway," Ivan added, "you want me to get a team of men and drag that ammo up? We could put it where your gunners can move it into the ammunition locker, under the aft big gun."

Lieutenant Wagner thought for a moment. "Sounds good — but watch yourselves. The Japs've got some sharpshooters over there who'd like nothing better than to pick off another victim."

Ivan frowned. "Another?"

"Yeah." Wagner nodded. "They got Summerfield."

"How bad?"

"It's not life threatening."

Still frowning, Ivan turned toward the door into the wheel-house. "Well, it's too bad Summerfield got wounded. We'll be careful. We've already figured out how we can get the ammo up to the main deck."

Wagner cocked his head to one side. "How?"

"We plan to crack the cases down below, then fire-brigade them up through the big ventilator air scoop, one sixty-round magazine at a time. The guy at the top, who'll probably be me, will lower them from the scoop entrance to the deck, which is protected by a good seven feet of landing-strip metal. From there, your boys can tote them to the munitions locker."

"Sounds good, Ivan. Tell Williams, on the aft three-incher, that I agree with the way you want to handle it. His crew is to put the ammo away. If he has any questions or suggestions, have him call me on the phone."

Ivan held up his index finger. "I have one last question. There appears to be a freight-train load down there. How many of those magazines do you want us to bring up?"

Wagner pursed his lips. "I think sixty-four should do it. That would be eight per tub, and we know where we can get more if we need it. Can you and your guys handle that many?"

"Sure, no problem at all." Ivan grinned. "See you later." The young Third Mate sprinted to the midship housing ladders that led to the main deck. Josh, on his way to the bridge, dodged out of Ivan's way as their paths crossed.

Josh, a wide grin on his face, walked into the wheel-house to report to the Captain. "The fire in number three hold is out. We were able to douse it before it really got going." He snapped his fingers to demonstrate how easily they'd conquered the blaze. "I decided I'd better go down, too. I wanted to make sure the boys did it right. We got it under control before the smoke and fire became a problem." He waved his hands expressively as he spoke. "Most of the three-by-five hatch boards fell down into the 'tween deck area. They landed on the hatch boards covering the lower hold with all that construction wood in it. We made sure all the fire was out where a couple of them broke through. Then we rearranged the boards that came from above in a sort of protective layer over the 'tween deck floor covers, just in case another mortar shell were to go down the now uncovered number three hold."

Captain Daly patted him on the back. "Good thinking, Josh. You're always thinking ahead. I like that."

Josh smiled at the welcome praise. But his glow of pride was cut short. The chatter of the 20mms broke the silence. That meant more mortars were on their way.

From the tree line on the beach two more *thunks* sounded. One of the shells made a direct hit on the midship housing rear bridge deck, where the empty, wooden potato bin sat, next to Sparks's quarters. The 20mm gun tub above his room shuddered from the blast, as did the men inside it. The shell hadn't missed them by more than five or six feet.

Investigating the area that had been hit, Captain Daly quickly determined there had been no casualties. On checking further he discovered a fire had broken out under gun tub number seven in the potato-bin rubble. Suddenly, Sparks's bed next to the open porthole burst into flames, too. Smoke drifted through the companionway leading to the radio shack, the bridge, the chart room, and both Lieutenant Wagner's and Captain Daly's quarters.

"Josh!" shouted the Captain, "Get men up here on the double to work the hose at fire station number four. We've got to get this thing stopped before the fire becomes serious!"

"Yes, Sir," he answered over his shoulder as he left the bridge at a full gallop. He raced to the crew mess, sure he could get a seaman or two to tackle the topside fire. He slid to a stop at the doorway.

Perkins, Gardner, and Esposito, trying to snatch a short break, had just poured some coffee. Josh motioned to them. "Come on. We've got another fire on the bridge deck. It's in Sparks's room and the potato bin under number seven gun. We have to get it out in a hurry. Thank God, you won't be facing any small arms fire where it's located."

Ivan, who'd reached the crew's mess four minutes earlier than Josh, had recruited two more men to join his previous five-man team. Both were Oilers and welcomed the opportunity to do any job that would keep them out of the scalding hot engine room. The eight of them would work in number five, hauling up ammo. He'd gathered them together to explain what they were going to do.

"You all know how a fire brigade works — one man handing to the next. That's how we're going to get those magazines up through the large air scoop ventilator shaft."

The men nodded their understanding.

"OK then, let's get busy."

After gathering the tools that he would need, Ivan led the group in a scurry on all fours to the fantail. Bunched together, they readied themselves to descend down the air scoop. Ivan called to the Coxswain in the 3-inch/50 tub. "Hey, Williams."

The gunner parted two of the metal mats that leaned against the two-by-four structure Chips had created as protection from sniper fire. "Yeah, whadda ya want?"

"I've got a cache of twenty millimeter ammo we found down in number five. Wagner said we could drop it here, and you guys would put it in the aft magazine munitions locker. OK?"

Williams' face, peeking between the parted mats, grinned widely. "Drop it, you say? You'll drop it? I assume you're kidding, but just in case you're not, let me tell you, you don't drop twenty millimeter, exploding-head ammunition."

Ivan waved his hand back and forth. "Yeah, yeah, I know. A bad choice of words. Just a figure of speech. Don't worry, we'll be careful."

Williams' head poked through a little farther. "Hang on a second, Ivan. I've got an idea I want to bounce off the Lieutenant." He turned away, clamping on his headset so he could use his phone. "Sir, since we have more ammo for the twenties coming up from below, we thought it'd be better to distribute it to the guns, rather than put it in storage. The guys must be getting pretty low by now, judging by all the firing we hear."

"Damn good idea, Williams, but can you do it without the risk of being picked off with sniper fire?"

"We're pretty sure we can. We'll move it the same way the merchant seamen do — on all fours, along the solid rail. As long as we keep our butts down they can't hit us."

"But how're you going to carry those magazines, when you're hunched over on all fours?"

"We'll only carry one sixty-round magazine at a time. We can strap it to our belly with our belts. We played around with this idea earlier, and it works." Williams chuckled. "There's no denying it's awkward as hell, but I'm sure we can do it . . . and I'm sure it'll be safe from sniper fire. Well, as safe as we can make it under the circumstances."

Lieutenant Wagner gave the go-ahead, then increased the volume of his voice. "Now, listen up, all you twenty-millimeter gunners. You heard the plan thus far. Here's the way to get your ammo. The aft big gun crew will get the magazines to the Armed Guard mess hall. You loaders will have to bring them up to your tubs from there."

He paused to take two deep breaths while he let the rest of the plan unfold in his mind. "Here's a list of rules to follow:

"Number One. Loaders, never leave your gunner unless he has a full or near-full magazine in his gun.

"Number Two. Only eight magazines to a tub.

"Number Three. Well . . . geeze, let's see . . . Oh, tubs eight and nine . . . you guys pick up your ammo where they're bringing it up. No need to schlep them to the mess hall only to have to bring them back to your guns.

"And Number Four. Be *careful*! Especially you guys up on number two and three guns. Stay low and crab-walk both ways along the solid rail the way Williams' crew is doing it."

He squinted his eyes and massaged the bridge of his nose. Had he forgotten anything important? Just one more thing to tell them.

"I guess the last thing would be regarding when to leave your stations to get the extra ammo. It'll be a half hour or so before it starts arriving at the mess hall. Any time after that when there's a lull in the mortar fire, like we're enjoying right now, would be a good time to make your move. But drop everything and get back to your stations on the double if another Charlie shows up. Your first duty is to man those guns. Then, as time permits, get the extra ammo."

Wagner cleared his throat. "Back to you, Williams. That's the game plan. Get your guys on it as soon as the ammo starts coming up from below."

"Aye, Sir. I'll get the merchant crew started right now." Williams removed the headset, then peered between the metal mats. What he saw made him smile. There was Ivan and his crew of handlers, all scrunched down behind the three-foot railing, their eyes closed, snatching a few minutes of rest before they set to work again. He made a noisy production of clearing his throat. "Hey, Ivan, the Lieutenant agrees, but with a slight change. Instead of stashing the ammo in our munitions locker, me and my boys are going to bring it to the Armed Guard mess hall. Men from the six forward twenties will pick it up from there to backup their dwindling inventory. The two tubs back aft will get theirs right from where you bring it up. All you guys have to do is get those magazines to the deck. We'll take it from there."

"Great! That'll save us some minutes." Ivan turned to his men. "You heard him. Let's get to it . . . one man at a time."

And one at a time it was, as the merchant seamen scurried up and over the metal runway plates and down the large ventilation scoop. When all were assembled on the 'tween deck, with flashlights lit, Ivan led the way to the ammunition cases they'd found earlier. He turned, facing the men. "Here's the routine. Kirk, since you've got the hammer and chisel, you'll be the one to open the wooden shipping containers. Be very careful your chisel doesn't hit any ammo, anywhere. I mean, be super careful!"

He made eye contact with each of the men. "That goes for all of you."

Each man nodded his understanding.

"Once open, you pull the magazines out of their cases. Two of you will alternate running the sixty-round magazine over to the rest of us who'll be up in the vent. Give it to the first man, who'll hand it to the next. It'll go up the shaft that way, one man handing to the one above him. I'll be at the top. I'll hand them down to the Navy gunners from the mouth of the scoop."

Ivan shone his light around, checking the look on each man's face to be sure he understood. "It sounds pretty simple to me, but if you have any — Holy *cow*! McDonald! Put out that friggin' match! There's no smoking down here! Damn . . . I didn't think I had to tell you guys that!"

He drew in several deep breaths as he waited for his heartbeats to return to normal. "I guess I'd better not assume anything, so . . . one more biggie. Twenty millimeter shells have an exploding head that blows up on contact with anything. Don't drop a case! Don't drop a magazine drum! Handle these sixty-round cartridges as if they were a two-day-old baby . . . with tender loving care." He waited to see if there were any comments. "Again I ask . . . do you have any questions?"

No one said a word.

Back on the bridge, Lieutenant Wagner flipped off his phone, dragged in a lungful of air and looked out the thick glass windows at the threatening beach area ahead. "It's comforting to know my guys won't run out of ammunition. I hate to think of how much damage those mortars might have done by now if we hadn't had the guns to break up their ability to zero in on us."

Captain Daly nodded in agreement. He rubbed his tired eyes once again. "Why do you suppose we haven't seen more airplane activity? I thought Negros had a reconnaissance airstrip."

Wagner halfway smiled. "That question has crossed my mind, too. It's possible that General MacArthur treated their field the same way he treated the one at Mindanao. According to a Navy Commander I talked to, it's rumored the Japs still have maybe as high as one hundred planes on the ground there."

"What did ol' Mac do at Mindanao?"

"He's a clever old fox. He hit all their gas storage areas with every type bomber he had under his command. Then the Navy moved in. Admiral Halsey assigned two wolfpacks of four subs each to blockade the island and prevent any tankers from bringing in new fuel for the grounded air force. If they did the same here, the Japs might feel we're not worth the gas it would take to do us in. They probably figure ground forces can do it fairly easily by themselves. Or . . . they might feel their valuable planes should be used on more important targets, like aircraft carriers. Why waste the gas on a small-potato Liberty ship that's permanently stuck on their shore?"

"Interesting thoughts, Wagner." The Captain waved his khaki shirt back and forth, trying to encourage some air to cool his body. "I guess time will tell how they choose to finish us off. Whatever it is, for the moment it appears they've decided to save their planes. Let me tell you, that doesn't hurt my feelings in the slightest."

The Captain walked out on the port-side bridge wing. Putting his binoculars to his eyes, he studied the area to the north. He searched for any sign of the two LSTs that were supposed to arrive by 1700 hours. Two dots appeared on the horizon. If they were the two expected ships, there was no way they'd get here by then. A chilling thought went through his mind. Suppose they were Jap destroyers called in from Manila Bay by the Negros garrison to seal the fate of the *Albert A. Robinson*. They could do it in a matter of minutes.

He shook that thought out of his head. He'd cling to the hope they were the LSTs.

A new possibility jumped to the forefront of his mind. If those were the expected craft, and they failed to pull the *Albert A.* free when they got here . . . or at the 2:00 a.m. high tide, would Pacific Command suggest they abandon ship? They could board the LSTs and head for deep water.

He mulled the thought over in his head. It was an interesting scenario, but a lot more time had to elapse before it could be thought about seriously. He realized a lot could happen between now and then — most of it bad. No matter, he'd remember to check periodically to see if the dots continued to travel in their direction.

Weary, he trudged back to the bridge. As he looked out the three small windows at the forward half of his ship, he caught sight of a stealthy movement. His gaze glued on the spot. The Mate and Boats snuck out from behind the winches of number one hold and scurried over to the winches for number two. Ten seconds later, the three seamen who'd been down in the hold working with the winch team, raced over and jumped in between the big winch motors where Boats and the Mate had taken cover.

The Captain smiled. They're good men, he thought. They're going to try to unload the Jeeps in number two also. Before long, two seamen raced out and hurriedly pulled off one of the centrally located three-by-five wooden hatch board covers, then turned and ran for protection between the two winches. He saw Jonesy stumble and fall before he reached the hiding place. Cash reached up and grabbed his hand, pulling him into the protected area.

"Oh, no," Captain Daly muttered. He'd seen the red streak on the hatch cover where Cash had pulled Jonesy to safety, and knew the seaman had been hit by sniper fire.

Chapter 12

ALONE ON THE BRIDGE, his officers busy elsewhere, Captain Daly yelled for Lieutenant Wagner. He knew the man would be in his usual spot on the starboard bridge wing. "I'm going below for awhile. One of the seaman working on hold number two just got whacked by a sniper. I want to see how badly he's hurt."

The Captain hurried toward the stairs down the back of the midship housing. On the way, he ran into the three seamen who had just finished dousing the flames in Sparks's quarters, and what was left of the empty potato bin. He approached them on the run. "If you're finished here just turn the water off and drop the hose. I've got a job for you." He dragged in a clean breath of air from outside the smoky companionway he'd just traveled through.

"Jonesy's been hit by a sniper. From where I was it looked bad. Right now he's with the Mate and Boats between the winches on number two. I want you to bring him to our temporary sick bay in the officers mess."

Perkins, the kid who always wore a pork-pie hat, and Gardner looked to Esposito, the seasoned veteran. He slapped them both on the back and barked, "You heard the Captain. Come on, you guys — move it!"

The three started down the inside ladder, Esposito in the lead.

"Hold it!" Captain Daly shouted to halt their progress. "I'll get the gunners to lay down cover for you. Wait till you hear them start to fire, then make your dash. You'll have to move fast — both ways. One of you will have to stay behind to take Jonesy's place down in the hold. You can decide between you which one that will be." He looked at his watch. "Wait to go until you hear several of the twenties on the port side cut loose. When that happens, in about two minutes, it'll be your cue to take off."

The seamen stood in readiness, shifting from foot to foot.

Noise shattered the brief quiet period when the four guns on the port side of the ship opened up a barrage, pounding the beach line with exploding shells. They directed their fire, not back where the mortar shots had come from, but up closer where they suspected the snipers had taken their positions.

The three men raced to the area where they'd been told the injured man would be.

Cash, feverishly working on Jonesy's leg, jumped with surprise when the three seamen slid in beside him. "What are you guys doing here?"

"The Captain saw Jonesy get hit. He sent us to get the kid to sick bay." Esposito studied the wounded man, noting his pallor, then turned to the Mate. "How is he?"

"I'm OK," Jonesy growled. He smiled, or at least he tried to. "My thigh's bleeding like a stuck pig, though. Ouch!"

Cash leaned away from the injured man to admire his work. He'd fashioned his shoelaces into a tourniquet, and had just made the band a little tighter. "There, that ought to help control the bleeding until you can get him to Doc Johnson."

Esposito nodded. "Looks good. You know, the guns you hear blazing away are our cover to get Jonesy out of here. We got to get him moving. How about it, Jonesy . . . a guy under each arm OK with you?"

Jonesy didn't have time to agree or disagree.

"Let's go, now!" Perkins didn't plan to wait around any longer. With

Esposito's help, he raised the seaman and slid his head under Jonesy's arm, his pork-pie hat still in place. Gardner promptly took his place on the other side. Esposito nodded to the two supporting their wounded shipmate. "Go! . . . Move it! Move it!"

They took off on the run, Jonesy dragging his wounded leg. The men remaining behind breathed a sigh of relief when the group disappeared into the midship housing. Although they'd heard sniper bullets hit the housing, they had missed their target. No one had been hit.

Cash looked at Esposito. "You here to take Jonesy's place down in the hold, Dante?"

"Yep, but you gotta tell me what to do."

One of the two seamen who'd been working with Jonesy poked the new man in the arm. "Do-na worry, Esposito, Remo and me'll tell ya what to do when we get down there," Gino said in his hoarse, squeaky voice. "We Paisanos, we work together, eh?"

Boats, eyes narrowed and serious, looked to each man. "Let me explain what's going to happen, so none of you clowns get hurt when you're down below."

With years of experience, and an expert at working the winches, he laid out his plan for removing the remaining hatch boards without exposing anyone else to sniper fire. "The Mate and I will feed the line down through the hole where you removed the one hatch board. You guys hook us up to the first Jeep." His hands went through the motions of the action he'd asked for. "Naturally, it's not going to fit through the three-by-five opening you made so, after you've got it hooked up, you three take cover in the corners. Be sure to protect yourselves. Cash and I'll bring the Jeep up like a battering ram. We'll use it to dislodge the cross beams over the hold." He paused. To make sure the three seamen understood his plan, he continued describing what would happen. "That means there'll be a dozen or so hatch boards coming down with a crash, as well as two, or maybe three, of the steel hatch beams. You don't want to be in the way of any of those."

Each man shook his head.

"No Sir, no way," muttered Gino.

"When you retreat to some protective corner, take a fire hose with you. The First Engineer assured me we have water pressure to all the hoses now. Spray those Jeeps as the covers and beams are falling, just in case one of them hits a Jeep just right to ignite its fuel tank."

Cash continued the warning. "With a little luck those beams will land somewhat crosswise on top of the Jeeps. Once we make a big enough hole to get the Jeeps out, we'll dump the one we used as a battering ram. Then we'll return the chain assembly so you can hook it up to any beams that are in your way. They'd be too heavy for the three of you to move."

All three men nodded their understanding.

Boats continued. "Once they're off to the side, we can start unloading the Jeeps." He finally smiled. "Now, if you happy Paisanos understood all the complicated hog wash, get your butts down that ladder and let's get to work."

Remo, Gino, and Dante scrambled down the mast house ladder to the 'tween deck level, where they waited for the winch cable to be lowered. The chug of the winches sounded, and soon the headache ball and cable found its way through the hole made by the removal of the single board. They hooked it up to the first Jeep, then took cover in the corner, well out of the way. Dante played the spray from the fire hose onto the Jeeps directly under the hatch opening. Like magic, Boats and Cash brought the Jeep up fast, battering the hatch beams.

Wooden hatch boards and large steel I-beams showered down into the hold, landing on the cargo of Jeeps. The three seamen scrambled over the wreckage and attached the chain assembly to the first steel hatch beam to be moved. Soon all beams were out of the way and the second Jeep attached to the winch cable. As it rose in the air, they cleared away the debris from another, making it ready to be lifted out. Jeep after Jeep left the darkness of the hold to briefly see the light of day, and then be dropped into a watery grave.

Captain Daly, standing on the bridge, put his binoculars to his eyes and looked up and down the beach area. "It's mighty quiet out there, Wagner," he said to the gunnery officer standing next to him. "Why do you suppose our uninvited Japanese guests have cut back on their mortar fire?"

"That's a good question, but their silence is a welcome opportunity for my gunners to oil their weapons. I gave them their orders to do just that, and do it fast. Who knows how much time they'll have before the guns are needed again." He removed his helmet and wiped the sweat from his forehead.

"But, back to your question . . . I'll ask a few of my own. Have we knocked out all their mortar crews, or did they only bring a limited number of mortar shells with them? Have they withdrawn because our twenty millimeter fire power has cost them too many casualties?" He shrugged his shoulders as if to say, "You're guess is as good as mine," adding, "I'd sure like to believe one of those scenarios, but I'm sure it's something else."

Wagner turned his head from side to side, then rotated it in a circle, obviously trying to relieve the tension of the last few hours. He frowned. "The last idea, the one of too many casualties, doesn't make sense. Under those circumstances they'd probably call in their air force to finish us off."

The Captain nodded. "It's hard to tell. We have no way of knowing, but I welcome the lull in the mortar fire. No doubt your men do, too." He trained his binoculars on the trees. "However, I don't think for a minute there are no sharpshooters in those forward trees, even though I can't see where they are. There's plenty of movement up close to the sand, I just can't pinpoint what it is. I'm sure the snipers are there, just waiting for a careless man to provide them with a target."

Wagner agreed. "I'll continue to remind my men periodically about that possibility, especially those bringing up new ammo to the gun tubs."

The Captain made another sweep of the beach with his binoculars, then let them hang down against his chest. "Why haven't we heard any machine-gun fire from those guys?"

Wagner grinned. "Because they're too smart."

Captain Daly frowned, confusion written on his face.

Before he could say anything, Wagner continued. "Firing machine-gun bullets two hundred and forty-some yards is very inaccurate; plus the machine-gun nest would be no match for three or four of our twenties pouring exploding-head shells at the telltale smoke of their discharge. No . . . they're just too smart to use machine guns against us."

"How about anything else in their arsenal? Do you think they might have grenade launchers?"

Wagner chuckled. "Again we lucked out. In their reported arsenal, the Japanese don't have one that will carry two hundred forty yards. At this point, mortar is their best weapon, until they can get something big, like a hundred and five howitzer, through the jungle. With that they can lob a big shell a long way."

"That's good news, I guess, but I have a feeling we're running out of time. The howitzer you refer to can't be that far away. If it gets in a solid clearing a mile or two away, it could do us in with the help of a local spotter. We'd have no way of knocking him out."

Wagner nodded. "I see you've been concerned about the possibility of the big gun, too."

The Captain turned and walked to the port-side bridge wing, Wagner following in his footsteps. "Here's another possible threat. A short time ago, through my binoculars, I spotted a couple of dots coming over the horizon from the North. They could be our LSTs, and then again . . . they could be Japs coming down from Manila Bay. I wonder if we could set up some sort of shielding on the flying bridge so the Signalman could contact them with the big blinker light. I'd like to know for sure if they're friendly." He raised his field glasses and studied the now larger dots. "They look like they're still better than two hours away, and heading directly toward us."

Wagner seemed to ponder the problem. "If it were night, we could do it right from here. The bridge wing is protected enough, but the hand-held small light doesn't have enough power to be readable that far in the daylight. Let me get some of my boys from the aft three-incher to work on it." He snapped on his phone system. "Williams, I need a couple of guys up here on the bridge. Send up Flags along with them." Flags was the name commonly given to the Navy semaphore and blinker-light operator. The Lieutenant turned to the Captain. "They should be able to work out some shielding method, so we can contact those approaching ships."

Wagner and the Captain walked back inside the wheel-house. It didn't take more than five minutes, if that, before two men bustled into the bridge.

Wagner frowned. "Brett, I thought I told Williams to send me more than just you and Flags."

"He couldn't, Sir. All the other men, plus a couple of merchant crewmen, are hauling twenty millimeter ammo to the Navy mess as fast as the seamen bring it up from below. Flags and I were working on that detail, too." He grinned. "Williams wasn't too happy to see us go."

"I guess not." Wagner chuckled. "Anyway, let me tell you about the project I have, then you can tell me if you two can handle it alone, or if you'll need some help."

After explaining about the approaching ships and the need to make communication with them, he said, "If you want to look through my binoculars at the forward gun you can see how they used the metal runway plates and C-clamps to form a shield from the snipers for Palmer." He slipped the strap over his head and handed the glasses to Flags. "Maybe you could do the same thing on the big light."

Flags studied the jerry-rigged shield that the crew of the 3-inch/50 had dreamed up for their protection.

While Flags looked through the glasses, Wagner suggested, "If you guys can't make a protective shield for Flags to stand behind," he pointed to the young sailor, "then perhaps you could remove the whole signaling light and take it back aft. You can plug it in back there . . . "

Flags lowered the binoculars and raised his finger to interrupt Wagner. "Sir, the big light can't be made portable. I mean, it can't be held by one person while I work the flaps. After turning on that umpteen-thousand-watt monster light, the thing gets hot as hell in a matter of a few seconds." He shook his head. "I think we should work on the shielding idea, unless we have two or three hours to come up with a plan to jerry-rig a holder back aft."

Wagner frowned. "I'm sorry to say, we don't have that kind of time. You've got twenty or thirty minutes to work out something. Let me know when you have a plan ready. I'll be here, in the bridge area."

Brett and Flags took off for the flying bridge ladder on the aft bridge deck. It took them up behind the protection of the ship's big smokestack. There they put their heads together, trying to come up with an idea for a shielding system for the big light.

"Aircraft approaching!"

The warning sounded from one of the gun tubs. All conversation stopped. Wagner looked at the Captain, his eyes tense, then went out on the starboard bridge wing and plugged in his phone system at the spotter station. He looked skyward in the direction of the motor sound.

Captain Daly strode briskly to his side. "Is it one of ours?"

Wagner shook his head. "Not unless we've started painting big red balls on the underside of our wings. There are two of them. One is the type Zero that attacked us before. The other is a bomber — a Mitsubishi G4M2. The flyboys call them "Bettys." That baby's capable of carrying a number of five-hundred pound bombs." He let his binoculars fall. "I'm afraid this is a seek-and-destroy mission . . . and we're the ones they plan to destroy."

Wagner took in two deep, fortifying breaths, straightened his shoulders, and looked directly at Daly. "And now, Captain, we know why their troops, with their mortars, pulled back. They knew air support was coming . . . or maybe they were the ones who ordered it."

Wagner paused briefly while he gathered his thoughts and decided what orders to give his men. He snapped on his phone, calling to all gun emplacements. "Be alert, men. Keep your eyes on the Zero, but keep your guns and your heads low. Don't forget about those snipers on shore while we deal with the Jap air force."

He closed his eyes for a brief moment. He wanted to prepare his young men for the fight ahead of them, get them ready to do battle without scaring them into immobility. He spoke calmly into his phone. "Let's consider the Zero for a moment. He's either along as cover for the bomber because they intercepted our request for air cover, or, and this is more likely, he plans to make a few strafing runs to try to knock out our twenty millimeter anti-aircraft guns. If he can do that, the bomber can come in lower, making his chances of hitting us much better." He took two more deep breaths as he offered up a silent prayer for the safety of his men. "Be sharp, guys! Things are about to happen."

Wagner watched the two planes approach. There was no doubt now that they were here to destroy the *Albert A.* In less than a minute, their plan jumped into action. The Zero banked heavily and approached for its run directly at the stern of the ship from almost a 30-degree angle. The pitch of its engine heightened as the pilot pushed his throttle into full speed. Puffs of smoke appeared from under his wings.

"Keep low, men! He's coming in with his twenty millimeter cannons blazing!" Wagner had no sooner given the warning than the chatter of the pilot's fuselage-mounted machine gun joined the answering *blat-blat-blat* of the ship's 20mms.

The .30-caliber machine guns of the Zero commenced blinking like a strobe light as they sent a deadly message to the gun tubs, spraying a hail of bullets their way. They clanked and ricocheted off the landing plates and decking, making almost as much noise as the *Albert A.*'s antiaircraft guns as they barked their answer to the uninvited Nips.

Wagner watched in amazement. The Zero was being met with fire from the aft three-incher and eight gun tubs shooting their 20s as fast as they could, yet no direct hits were scored. There'd been a lot of near misses, but, with the amount of bullets flung into the air, you'd think one of them would have hit the daring Zero.

About 200 yards off the stern, the Zero made a sharp climb and peeled off to the left. "Good work, men. I guess he decided he didn't want to get any closer to our guns," he said into the communication system. Williams, on the aft three-incher, got off one last round as the crafty pilot flew out of range.

The Lieutenant knew it was time to see what damage they might have endured. "How we doing out there? If there are any wounded, let me know." He waited, holding his breath. When no reports of casualties came from his gunners, he muttered a heartfelt prayer of thanks.

He hesitated just a moment before he felt ready to speak. "Those guys up there are crafty. Whatever they're setting up for, you can be sure they've done it before and no doubt had success with it. All I can say is . . . stay alert!"

Wagner watched the two planes, obviously in communication with each other. They banked off the stern. Good move on their part, he thought. It'll give the Betty a longer target in his sights.

Once more he spoke to his men. "The Zero is positioning himself for another run. And it looks like the bomber will be coming on this pass, too. He'll be traveling about two hundred yards above the Zero. They've been known to use this tactic before . . . and successfully; but we're going to fool them."

The Zero broke first, once again trying to silence at least one of the 20s. Barring that, he apparently wanted to draw all the fire power his way, giving the slower large bomber flying over his head a better chance to make a low enough run to hit his target. The pitch of the Zero's engine screamed a warning as it commenced its dive.

Wagner yelled, "Ignore the Zero. The bomber is coming in this time. Go for it!"

The stream of .30-caliber bullets from the Zero bounced off the cement gun tubs. Some ricocheted around in the enclosures where the loaders were crouched low behind the shooters. The Nip pilot seemed to be in deadly earnest in his attempt to knock out the gun emplacements. The gunners ignored his presence, as they'd been ordered, and concentrated their fire on the Mitsubishi bomber.

Flying through a curtain of 20mm shells, and two more close bursts from the three-incher, the Betty unloaded its first big bomb. It narrowly missed the ship, exploding alongside, some 20 to 30 feet from the midship housing and opposite the engine room. The concussion of the blast underwater rocked the *Albert A.* She shuddered and shook like a 12-point earthquake. The men not near anything they could grab ended up on their knees. Mud, sand, and water geysered up, covering Wagner and the gun crew on the starboard side of the midship housing.

"I don't believe it!" Wagner vigorously shook his head. "That lucky son of a bitch. He just experienced another damn miracle for the Nips. We loaded the sky with bullets, and I didn't see one meaningful hit on that lucky bastard." He scanned the sky. "I see the Zero, but where in hell did the bomber go?"

Chapter 13

PALMER, THE pointer on the big forward gun, answered Lieutenant Wagner's question. "He continued straight ahead over our bow. He disappeared over that first hill dead ahead. We got off one shot that damn near ran up his tail pipe, but it didn't burst until it was a hundred yards or more in front of him."

Captain Daly had watched the last run by the two planes from the bridge wing. He'd not said a word during this time, keeping silent so that he wouldn't distract Wagner. The whistle from the engine room sounded from the communication tube. He rushed to answer it. "This is the Captain speaking. What do you want?"

"Yeesus *Christ*!"

The Captain smiled. "What is it, Chief?"

"Vot's going on up there? Did ve get hit? Are ve to abandon ship?"

"Hold it, Chief. We weren't hit. I'll admit it was close, a near miss right alongside the engine room." The Captain cleared his throat. "Did you sustain any serious damage?"

"Yeesus *Christ*, I thought the bulkhead on the starboard side vas going to cave in. Ve have several ruptured lines and some new steam leaks. I hear vater coming in through cracks in the outer layer." He paused to get the hacking cough under control. "I'm going up now to see if I can tell how much vater is involved. Let's hope the bilge pumps can keep up with it. If not, and it reaches the fire box, we're all through." Another coughing jag hit him, this one more severe than the last.

Captain Daly waited impatiently for the coughing to cease. "Chief, we've got a Zero and a bomber up here looking to polish us off. That blast you felt so hard could have done it, if it had actually hit us and not just landed alongside. Those Nips are still up there preparing to make another run at us. Keep your fingers crossed . . . and don't worry. If we have to abandon ship we'll let you know." He heaved a big sigh. "Being on the rocks like we are, you don't have to be afraid we might sink." He sighed again. "If the truth be known, Chief, you're in the safest part of the ship right now."

"Yeesus *Christ*, dats not a very comforting thought, Cap'n. I got to get back to vork and get those pipes sealed. Keep us informed, Cap'n. We need to know what's going on topside."

"Will do, and you do whatever you have to, Chief, to repair those leaking pipes — and keep a full head of steam in the main boilers." The Captain snapped the whistle button closed on the talking tube and headed for the bridge wing where Lieutenant Wagner stood, directing his gunners.

A few minutes earlier, down in the galley, Cookie had tilted the large, stainless steel pot on the edge of the stove. It brimmed with a new batch of Bully Beef Borscht. Raul, the Filipino mess man, stood next to the stove, a smaller portable pot in his hand. He'd been running the hot, nourishing soup to various points on the ship all day. It was time to deliver some more.

"Now hold the bloody pot still, and don't let go if a few drops splash on your hands. Ready?"

Raul nodded.

"Here it comes." Cookie grunted as he tipped the heavy pot over to fill the smaller one.

Ka B*oom*!

At precisely that instant the powerful bomb from the Betty exploded a few feet from the starboard side.

The ship lurched. Galley pots and pans, ladles and spoons, flew off their racks and across the room.

Cookie fell back. The hot BBB cascaded over the edge of the pot and splashed, in a mini wave, down his bare legs.

Raul dropped the smaller pot and instinctively reached out to stop his fall. His hand landed on the stove. A sound like sizzling bacon on a hot griddle, told the story of what had happened before his scream of pain filled the room. It mingled with Cookie's many four-letter words, interspersed with a number of "bloodies."

Cookie continued yelling, "son of a friggin' bloody bitch!" many times in succession as he wiped the thick stew from his legs with a wet towel, trying hard not to remove his boiled skin. Finally, jumping up on the drainboard, he put his feet in the sink. He turned on the cold water and splashed enough of it down his legs to remove the soup from the badly burned areas.

Once he'd taken care of himself, he beckoned to Raul, who stood doubled up in pain, holding his burned hand.

Cookie removed his legs from the water, jumped down from his perch and walked toward his young helper. "Let me see it," he ordered.

Raul held out his hand, palm up, his eyes filled with pain.

Cookie frowned. "Dat's a nasty one, all right." He paused for a few seconds. "I guess we're not sinking. Come on, let's go see Doc and Elijah. Maybe they can fix us both up." Cookie limped out of the galley and down the companionway to the temporary infirmary, Raul trailing him like a lost puppy.

Back on the flying bridge, Lieutenant Wagner made slow, 360-degree turns, trying to locate the whereabouts of the bomber. He opened up his sound-powered mike. "It looks like the Zero is setting up for another strafing run. It's possible one of you guys put a shot into the Betty and he decided to head for home and some needed repairs. One of your twenties breaking the skin and exploding inside could have done some serious damage." He made another slow, complete turn, making sure the bomber hadn't made another appearance.

"What's the Zero doing now, Wagner?" The Captain had been watching it. It seemed to start a run, then bank off, circle around and start another one.

"I don't know. I suspect one of these times he'll come in at us for real, but, for the moment, he's playing with us for some reason."

Wagner made another 360-degree turn, his binoculars gripped tightly in his hands while he searched the sky for any sign of the bomber. Where was the damn thing?

Still searching the sky, he tried his best to answer the Captain's question. "We know the Zero is capable of carrying two bombs. He might be thinking of making a bombing run of his own."

"Could he be waiting for more Zeroes or more bombers?" The Captain paced back and forth on the bridge wing.

"I haven't the foggiest idea what his plan is, or why he's making these make-believe runs. I'm sure he's not chicken, so he must be trying to confuse us."

"He's doing a damn good job of that."

"You're right." Wagner dropped his binoculars for a moment to look at Daly. "You'll notice, he always pulls up before he gets into our antiaircraft range. He's playing some sort of game." He tilted his helmet back and mopped the sweat from his high forehead to keep it from running into his eyes. "I wish to hell I knew what it was."

From the stern, the pitch of the Zero's motor turned into a scream as the pilot gave it full throttle.

"OK, boys, he's coming in. He means business this time. Let's get him!" Wagner encouraged his crew.

Every gunner on the ship trained his sights on the approaching plane, waiting for him to get into firing range. The aft three-incher fired first, its shell exploding close to the fighter.

As the Zero got within the range of its guns, the pilot commenced firing, strafing the *Albert A.* The ship's 20s had aimed carefully, but had not begun firing. This time luck was on her side. Before any of the guns cut loose with their loud cannon fire, the drone of the bomber's two motors reached the ears of the gunners. The huge plane approached directly over the trees, dead on the bow of the ship.

Wagner turned to see the Betty coming in low. He yelled to his gunners. "Turn around! Get the bomber! He's coming in over the bow!" Even though the strafing fire from the Zero sent bullets clanking, banging, and clattering across the deck and against the metal strips protecting the ammunition hold, Wagner's orders were heard loud and clear in each gun tub.

All guns turned 180 degrees, exposing the backs of the gunners to the Zero's strafing. Ignoring that fact, the guns blazed away at the nearing Betty. Wagner swallowed when he saw it release two large bombs. "Hit the deck!" he yelled, then dove into the wheel-house. He brushed against Captain Daly, almost knocking him down, as he entered on the fly.

Both bombs exploded in the rocky surf a few yards off the starboard bow, just opposite the number two gun tub. The ship lurched up a full five feet at the bow, like it had hit a mine. A geyser of water, mud, and rocks covered the number two tub and the three-inch/50 crew. The concussion of the explosion, and the sudden upward and sideways lurch of the deck lifted them off their feet and dropped them on the deck. One by one they picked themselves up from where they'd fallen.

The ship rocked slowly, then settled down in the rocky surf again.

Captain Daly felt a sliding motion as the ship settled back in the rocks, followed by a mysterious grinding and crunching. He got up off his knees where the blast had knocked him and ran over to the mechanical engine room signaling handle. Whipping it back and forth first to make sure the bells all rang down below, he settled the arrow in Full Astern and crossed his fingers. His eyes glittered with hope when he turned to face Wagner

The Lieutenant, still down on one knee, drew his brows together in a look of confusion. "What are you doing?"

"Didn't you feel that motion? Hear that grinding? Maybe, with a little luck, those two bombs might have moved us off the big rocks, or at least split the ones we were wedged on." He held up one hand with fingers crossed. "We'll soon know." He took three steps to the tube that communicated with the engine room and blew into it hard.

Almost immediately Svenson, the Second Engineer, gruffly answered. "Yeah, yeah, we're cranking it over to Full Astern now. We got troubles, though. Whatever just hit us caught the Chief coming down the ladder. He took a hell of a header down a full flight, landing in a heap on the iron grate below. I gotta go see if I can help him. He's just laying there, at the bottom of the ladder, unconscious." Svenson paused, his voice a little shaky, then added, "But you can rest assured . . . you're in Full Astern now."

The tube snapped shut. The Captain knew how upset Svenson must be. The Engineer hadn't even bothered to find out who he'd been talking to. Daly, his stomach doing a slow roll, knew the feeling. He whispered into the dead tube, "Take care of my good old friend . . . please take care of him."

He stepped away from the tube, the concern his heart felt written on his face. How much damage could the Chief sustain? A fall from that height, down the iron ladder to the oil-slick metal floor of the engine room, could put a serious hurt on a man of his advanced years. He prayed it wouldn't be too bad.

The big ship trembled as the screw began to churn the water in earnest. More grinding noises sounded from up forward.

Palmer called out, "We're moving . . . we're *moving*!"

The Captain grinned as cheers went up from everyone within earshot of the welcome news.

Lieutenant Wagner, back out on the starboard wing of the bridge where he had better visibility, trained his gaze on the two Jap planes.

Captain Daly, grinning from ear to ear, rushed to his side. "Did you hear that, Wagner? We're pulling free from the rocks!"

Wagner never took his eyes off the enemy. "Yeah, I heard, but at the moment I'm more interested in those two Nips out there. It looks like they're preparing to make another run at us." When he'd made his beeline for the protection of the bridge, he'd thrown down his head set. Now, he picked it up and adjusted it. He cleared his throat before sending his orders to his crews. "Men, look alive out there! Those two bozos aren't done with us yet. The Zero is getting ready to make another pass. If the Betty pulls in behind him, ignore the Zero. We can't let that bomber get in close. He won't miss a third time!"

The Zero banked and again started his run from the stern. Diving at almost a 35-degree angle, his motor screaming at full throttle, the pilot seemed more determined than ever to knock out the *Albert A.*'s tenacious return fire. Sweeping in with his guns spewing smoke and raining lead down on the gun tubs, he seemed dedicated to the annihilation of the stubborn Yankee gunners. Their resistance, and the power from their guns, kept thwarting the bomber's ability to get close enough to destroy the ship. He appeared bent on changing all that.

Wagner watched closely, his eyes bouncing back and forth from the fast-approaching Zero to the slower Betty. He hollered into his phone, "The bomber isn't coming on this run. You guys concentrate on the Zero. Let's get him! I'll keep my eye on the bomber."

His gunners stood firm. Martinez, Perry, and the rest kept their fingers on their triggers, sending a stream of fire power at the Zero. Williams, on the aft three-incher, exploded two close shots at the screaming enemy aircraft as it approached.

The AA guns belched out smoke and bullets like a kid with a pea shooter and a mouthful of peas. Wagner's chest swelled with pride. Even though the Nip's bullets and exploding 20s bounced in the tubs, ricocheting around the gunners and their loaders, still the men never wavered. He knew all eyes were fixed on the Zero and its reckless approach.

Before reaching the *Albert A.*, the Zero sharply veered off to the right. Black smoke poured out of its fuselage. The bomber, meanwhile, chose to stand its ground far out of range of the ship's guns. Lieutenant Wagner, wary of what the Betty might do, kept his eye on it.

Through his headphones he heard the cheers that went up from the gunners. They shouted insults at the crafty pilot who had evaded their previous efforts to bring him down. "We got him! We *got* him!" The cry went up from more than one tub. "Go on home and lick your wounds, you SOB!" Still another crew added, "Mark one Jap flag on our smokestack!"

The Lieutenant shook his head at the banter, laughter, and insults passing from tub to tub, as the weary men watched the smoke trail the wounded Zero left behind. Wagner followed its progress as it made a large, low circle. When it went down, they'd still have the bomber to contend with.

He'd better prepare his men, get them sharp again. "OK, you guys. The Zero's probably heading for the beach so he can ditch close to shore. I know you want to watch your first kill splash down, but let's not lose sight of that bomber up there. He's the big threat, now."

Wagner took one more look at the wounded Zero, then trained his binoculars on the Betty. "Williams, let's send a message to our friend out there. We want to let him know we're watching him. Set a shell for long range — no, let's make that two. Try to make them closer together this time. I want him to continue to think we have modern AA equipment on board."

"Aye, Sir."

Wagner knew most of his men would keep their eyes on the Zero. He divided his attention between the crippled fighter and the lumbering bomber. The Zero continued its slow turn, never gaining any altitude. He imagined each of his men now anxiously waited for the plane to hit the water, expecting it to happen at any moment. But . . . it didn't. After making a complete circle, the Zero straightened out, coming down the beach from about four miles away. The plane headed directly for the side of the ship, about 30 or 40 feet off the water.

Wagner's stomach jumped into his throat when he heard the pitch of the Zero's engine increase. He switched his field glasses to the wounded plane. It didn't take him long to discern the pilot's intentions. "Men! That son of a bitch doesn't plan to ditch. He's not through with us yet!" He let the binoculars fall against his chest, where his wildly beating heart jumped around. "He doesn't intend to strafe us. He wouldn't be coming in so low, or from the side of the ship, if that were his plan. He has a more glorious mission on his agenda." He took a deep breath and swallowed. "Williams, cancel that long shot. Go for the Zero! The rest of you hold your fire 'til he gets in range!"

"Son of a *bitch*!" Martinez, in the gun tub over Wagner's head, uttered the oath everyone felt.

Wagner listened to the four-letter words dance along the phone line. His crews had obviously realized what the pilot's intentions were. Anyone who listened to the hourly news broadcasts piped into the mess halls had heard of the new "weapon" the Japs had recently employed with such success. *Kamikaze*! A suicide ram into the ship that has disabled his plane. The tactic had taken out, or at least badly damaged, many ships in the last three months. That had to be the single thought on the mind of the Zero pilot.

Wagner knew how each man must feel at this moment — a mirror of his own frantic thoughts. Like him, every gunner and every loader knew this was it. The game of war, and the stakes involved, had moved to the highest point. Now the chips were on the table in one last winner-take-all hand. Either you get him, or he gets you.

Each man would draw on his reserve of courage. His breathing would grow deeper. His heart would race, as adrenaline flowed through his veins.

His lungs would strain to drag in more air. Then all his training would take over conscious thought, as each man would focus on the enemy plane.

Wagner spoke into the phone, his voice strong with emotion. "In case any of you guys haven't realized that Nip's intentions, let me enlighten you. You are looking at a Kamikaze pilot. He's going to try to ram us on the starboard side, probably at the water line, to make sure we sink." He paused, to take in a deep breath and give his words time to sink in.

He didn't want his voice to falter.

He took another fortifying breath to steady it.

"If you don't have a near-full cartridge in your guns, jettison the pack that's there and reload with a full sixty-shell drum, now! We have to bring him down!"

He struggled to get his ragged breathing under control.

"We have to bring him down!"

Pause.

"You hear me? If he hits us near the munitions hold, we're finished!"

His voice cracked momentarily.

"We have to bring him down before he can get to the ship!"

Standing on the starboard wing of the bridge right under tub number four, Wagner kept his eyes on the struggling plane. Frowning, he swallowed, then chewed his lower lip. Could the pilot keep the Zero aloft long enough to reach the *Albert A.*? He cautioned his men again. "Those responsible for removing the spent magazines and reloading — be fast! Faster than you've ever been in your life — because your life may depend on it now."

The 3-inch/50 let go first with a long-distance shot. The preset shell exploded about a hundred yards or so in front of the approaching Zero. The gunners, their weapons now reloaded, trained their sights on the threatening enemy.

Wagner took it all in. Everything seemed to shift into slow motion. Seconds passed that felt like minutes. The plane came closer. He judged the distance. It's close enough now, he thought, and gave the order . . . "This is it, guys. Start firing!"

Gun tubs two, four, six, and eight on the starboard side threw out a blanket of bullets at the oncoming Zero. Tubs three and nine joined in when he got close enough so that they could fire without hitting the personnel in tubs two and eight. Because the aircraft stayed only 30 or 40 feet off the water, tubs five and seven, on the port-side midship housing, had to hold their fire lest they hit personnel in numbers four and six, which loomed directly in the path of the low-flying Zero.

By this time, no one watching had any doubt of the Jap's intentions. His cannons and machine guns were silent. His sole objective was to keep his flying missile of destruction in the air and on target. Wagner shook his head. The Japanese pilots were fanatics. He knew the man in that plane believed if he sunk the *Albert A.* as a trophy to his Emperor, he'd earn eternal life for himself. He'd become a Kamikaze — a Divine Wind for his god.

Captain Daly watched the oncoming plane through the chart room porthole. The chatter of 20mm-cannons laid down a continuous barrage at the oncoming plane. It seemed impossible it could stay in the air a minute longer. But, the damn thing kept coming.

Since no strafing fire came from the Zero or the snipers on shore, the loaders stood alongside the 20s instead of crouched down to shield themselves from bullets. They'd placed a new magazine at their feet, ready to insert it the second the spent clip was removed. The gunners, strapped into the harness, desperately tried to keep their sights on the Zero. The recoil from the cannons shook them until their teeth rattled. The continuous fire caused the guns to get blistering hot. Smoke coming off the recently oiled barrels and recoil mechanisms became so thick the gunners couldn't be sure their sights were on the Zero at all times. Even so, their fire continued at an unrelenting pace.

Miraculously, the Zero kept coming. Five hundred yards away, his engine, coughing and sputtering, belched out a trail of smoke. It didn't deter him. He stayed at full throttle, on a beeline for the ship.

Chapter 14

LIEUTENANT WAGNER shook his head in disbelief. How could the Jap keep the plane in the air? One of his wing gas tanks had been hit, and fuel was flowing out of it, but by some perverse miracle, there'd been no explosive fire. How much good luck could the bastard have? "How in hell can you possibly continue to elude a significant hit," he muttered. "With the fire power we're directing at you, you should be history, you lucky son of a bitch!"

Several new puffs showing hits on his wings sent strips of aluminum shaking in the wind. Another shell removed his antenna. One more caused his wheels to drop down.The plane shook and wobbled, but never strayed from its course. The pilot had taken aim on the starboard side of the midship housing . . . no doubt at the

waterline. Unless they could bring him down, it looked like he would reach it.

Martinez, strapped in the gun over Wagner's head, shouted as he poured every bullet the 20 under his command could fire. "G-go-o-o d-down-n-n y-you s-son-n of a b-bi-itch! Go downnnn! Damn y-you, g-g-o-o d-down-nn!" The recoil from his cannon shook his body so violently, he couldn't help but stutter as his teeth clacked together.

Gun tub number six, just 40 feet away, reloaded in record time. Smoke and flames leaped from the barrel as Perry, the gunner, yelled, "Die, you bastard, *die*!" Thick beads of sweat dripped from his forehead. He blinked his eyes, but the salty moisture kept running into them, stinging and blurring his vision. He couldn't take the time to wipe it away. Squinting, then blinking his eyes rapidly to focus his foggy eyesight, he kept the trigger of his gun pulled back. "You friggin' son of a bitch, hit the water!"

Gun tub number eight, next to the number five hold where the ammo was stored, had a problem. Gordy Durks, probably the youngest member of the Armed Guard, served as a loader. He stood by the blazing gun, sobbing and shaking with fear. And then the magazine went dry.

Maddock, a veteran gunner, yelled, "Come on, ditch that mother and reload me, you crybaby!"

Durks quickly tossed the empty magazine, all the while sniffling and moaning like a ten-year-old who'd just witnessed his new, shiny bicycle being backed over by a truck. With shaking hands, he grabbed a full pack, but it slipped from his sweaty fingers and bounced across the gun tub floor. He stood frozen, staring at it.

"Don't just look at it! If it was going to explode, it would have already," growled Maddock. "Get it in the gun! Damn it, get it in the gun!"

Durks picked it up and shoved it in the breach, but it wouldn't latch. "I-I think s-something bent when I dropped it … I-it w-won't snap in!"

"Well, toss it over the side and get a new one, for Pete's sake. *Now*, damn it, not next week!"

Durks managed to get the new cartridge in and latched.

Immediately, Maddock had the gun spitting out its killing ammunition at the now all-too-close Zero. "Hit the surf, or eat my bullets, you lucky little sucker!"

Young Durks crumbled in a heap to the floor of the tub, completely spent, both mentally and emotionally. He couldn't stop the tears that coursed down his cheeks, or his wailing sobs.

The Divine Wind kept coming, his motor missing badly. His sights were definitely set on the middle of the ship. The distance lessened to a hundred yards.

Both Lieutenant Wagner and Captain Daly stared at the approaching plane. They stood in what appeared to be the target area. Even if the pilot were dead, even if his motor stopped this second, it seemed likely he'd hit the *Albert A.* somewhere amidships. Realizing the danger, they both ran for cover.

Wagner yelled, "He's going to hit us!" as he raced across the face of the bridge. He dove through the open bridge door to the port-side wing. His mind blanked out, as if frozen in time. He hit the deck, slithering on his hands and knees against the bulkhead, his helmet hitting it with a clank.

Captain Daly ran straight out the chart room door and down the companionway toward the radio shack, some ten steps away.

Ka B*oooooom*!

The Zero hit with a tremendous, ear-splitting explosion, right between the chart room and the Captain's quarters. Flaming debris flew through the air, everywhere.

The concussion of the plane's impact, plus the exploding fuel tank and probably one or maybe two small bombs, slammed Sparks against the typewriter table so hard, it's floor bolts pulled out of the cement deck. He wound up in a heap in the corner of the shack atop the turned over wooden table.

A body came hurtling into the room, engulfed in a fire ball that filled the shack in less then a second. It glowed red at first, then blinding white, with no images and no shadows.

Instinct told Sparks, "I've got to get some air." Scrambling over the typewriter table he couldn't see, but could feel against his shins, he reached the open porthole. He thrust his head out and dragged in two big gulps of air. The heat surrounded him, so intense he felt seared, as if he'd been hit by a flame-thrower.

He dragged in another big breath before pulling his head back inside the room. The solid wall of the fire ball had disappeared as fast as it had occurred, leaving every scrap of paper in the room either glowing red on its edges or on fire. Even the ragged ends of his khaki cutoffs and shirt sleeves glowed red. He quickly patted out the smoldering areas with his hands.

He looked about the room. The uniform on the prone body that had flown into the radio shack smoked. Sparks grabbed the five-gallon jug of distilled water for the emergency batteries. He drenched the still figure from head to toe, putting out all the glowing areas. He doused the fire in the trash can and the log book paper with the leftover water. Coughing uncontrollably, he realized he now had a more serious problem . . . the need for air.

Smoke billowed into the room, so thick he could barely see. Breathing became almost impossible. He heard the crackle of the fire that engulfed the area leading to the chart room and Captain's quarters. That's where all this smoke is coming from, he thought. He dropped the empty water bottle. Gasping and gagging, he scrambled once more to the open porthole. He gulped in air, one breath after another, trying to clear his lungs and stop coughing. Getting it, if not under control, at least slightly better, he took one more deep breath and held it. He climbed back over the upended typewriter table, grabbed the ankles of the unconscious man, and dragged him out of the room on his stomach and down the companionway toward the back exit.

Outside the shack he took a better look at the victim. "My God, it's the Captain!" He tugged on the prone figure until his lungs screamed for oxygen. He could find none. At the doorway he let go of the Captain's feet, took five steps out on the rear deck and fell to his knees. Three gulps of air later, although he still coughed uncontrollably, he stepped back inside, firmly grabbed the Captain's shoulder and rolled him onto his back. Once more, getting a grip on his ankles, he backed up, dragging the limp man over the threshold and out the door to fresh air — as fresh as could be found. He couldn't get away from the smoke that hung in the air from all the fires that had sprung up.

Sparks heard frantic shouting from almost every fire station. Seamen yelled to each other as they unwrapped the hoses.

"Starboard lifeboats are gone!" cried one man.

"Oil-soaked canvas on hold number four is on fire!" shouted another.

"Deck officers' quarters are on fire!" came from someone else.

Then a voice from one of the gun tubs over his head yelled, "The tarp over the flying bridge and some of the wood planking is on fire!"

Smoke poured out of all the open portholes on this deck, and from the exit Sparks had just come through. He wiped the tears streaming from his smoke-irritated eyes. His mind filled with dire thoughts of what might be happening. *The fires in the Captain's quarters and the chart room were spreading fast. Sparks knew that the inch-thick plywood bulkhead would make good fuel. And he knew that the seamen had better get to it before they lost the whole deck.*

Cries came from the wounded and burned victims in the gun tubs on the starboard side of the midship housing where the Kamikaze had hit. The loaders had both dived for cover in the deepest parts of the gun tubs at the time of impact. They got away from the intense heat of the resulting fireball.

The gunners hadn't been so lucky. Strapped in, they had continued to fire at the oncoming Zero, shredding it into an incendiary flying missile 25 yards before it had finally crashed into the midship housing. Helmets and life jackets had protected some parts of their bodies, but arms, faces, and legs had been exposed. The two gunners in tubs four and six had suffered serious burns.

Sparks cocked his head to listen. Had he heard a weak voice calling out? There it was again. The sound came from the port side. He strained to make out the words of the garbled cry. He heard them clearly this time. "Man overboard! Somebody throw us a line!" He headed toward the sound, but then a new peril presented itself.

The destructive explosion on the ship had spurred the Japanese ground forces to resume their attack. They lobbed a new volley of mortar shells, one after another, at the *Albert A. Robinson* as she slowly slipped off the rocks. Sparks returned and ducked down next to the prone Captain. What the Nips had thought was a permanently beached ship seemed to be slipping away. Perhaps this had prompted the new attack. Or maybe, with all the fires on board, they thought there would be no returning gunfire from the 20s. Whatever the reason, something had inspired them to launch this new, all-out mortar barrage. The snipers had joined in too, sending their deadly messages all over the ship. Shell after shell was pumped at the slowly moving Liberty.

Lieutenant Wagner, still on the port side bridge wing, climbed the ladder to the flying bridge and jumped into the number five gun tub, plugging in his means of communication. "I'll keep my eyes on the Betty . . . you guys take care of those mortar installations — now!"

All guns turned toward the beach. Again, the 20s sent a stream of bullets whenever and wherever a telltale puff of smoke would betray the location of a hidden mortar. The three-incher on the bow joined in. The shoreline became so covered in smoke that Wagner knew the gunners must be having a hard time detecting the puff from enemy mortar from one of their own exploding 20mm shells.

The *Albert A.* had definitely slipped off the rocks. She moved slowly — but she moved — away from the beach. The troops on Negros could see it, too, and in their haste, before the ship got out of range, their accuracy had suffered. Wagner thanked God for that. Even so, they kept the mortars coming. Most landed in the water, but not all. And the crack of sniper fire never let up. The Japanese sharpshooters attempted to pick off any seamen who went to the aid of an injured buddy, or who manned a hose to fight the fires.

Wagner could find no fault with his men. The gunners aboard the *Albert A.* did their best to quell the mortar barrage. He knew the muzzles of their 20s were smoking hot, yet they pumped magazine after magazine at the enemy on shore.

Sparks checked over the Captain one more time. As far as he could see, there was nothing more to be done. The Captain seemed to be breathing normally, but hadn't regained consciousness. The large gash on his head atop the lump he'd gotten when he'd hit the bulkhead continued to ooze blood, as all head wounds seem to do. Satisfied the Old Man was in a comparatively safe location on the back bridge deck, he mentally questioned himself. *Should I get someone to take care of the Captain, or should I see if I could assist whoever went overboard?*

Just then he heard the sound of men scrambling up the ladder. Josh stepped onto the deck, followed by three seamen ready to fight the bridge deck fire.

Sparks looked up. "Josh. Am I glad to see you!" he rasped, his voice almost a whisper. "I dragged the Captain out here." He pointed to the limp figure laying on the deck. "He's unconscious, but he seems to be OK otherwise. I did what I could for him."

Josh knew Captain Daly had been in the chart room when the Kamikaze hit. He was glad the Captain had made it out. He turned to the men following him. "The smoke in there is too thick to breathe. One of you, take a big breath, grab the hose, and get in there. In thirty seconds, one of you other guys fill your lungs, then go relieve him." He pointed at the first man. "He'll need some air by then. In another thirty seconds, the last man will go in." He indicated the third seaman. "Keep alternating like that. Whatever you do, keep the hose on that fire!"

Sparks put a hand on Josh's shoulder to get his attention.

Josh turned around.

"Did you know there are some men overboard on the port side? They keep calling. I don't think anyone is tending to them."

Just then, a lull in the gunfire let a faint cry drift up to Sparks and Josh. "Man overboard . . . for Chris' sake — someone throw us a line!"

"Since the ship's moving, the men are being left behind," Sparks concluded.

Josh nodded, then directed his attention to the three seamen. "You guys take care of that fire. I gotta take care of whoever went over the side." He headed down the ladder.

Sparks looked up to see three Navy men coming down from the flying bridge deck. Two of them stepped gingerly. "Can I help you guys?"

"Nah, we'll make it," Clark answered as he, Perry, and Martinez climbed cautiously backwards down the ladder. "Perry and Martinez got some bad burns. I'm taking them down to the infirmary."

"Better go down the outside ladder," Sparks pointed out, "The inside area is choking with smoke.

Josh ran down the ladder to the boat deck, past the port side lifeboat. A lot of smoldering debris remained on the deck from the lifeboat that had taken the direct hit earlier. He sprinted past the burning embers, up the ladder to the port-side bridge wing where a two-man cork and canvas life raft was kept. He pulled the belaying pin that held it in place. Over the side it went.

He whirled around and raced back down the ladder. Snatching a life preserver from under the port wing, he peered over the rail to see if anyone in the water couldn't swim. Two men were already swimming toward the raft he'd just released. He didn't see anyone else, so he dropped the ring in his hand onto the deck.

"Damn it to hell," he muttered when he became aware of another problem. The ship had picked up speed, leaving the two men in the water many yards behind. He turned when he heard a noise behind him.

Cash clambered up the ladder to the boat deck, two stairs at a time. In between breaths he yelled, "I need a man on the wheel . . . get me a helmsman . . . someone . . . *now*!"

"Hey, Cash," Josh yelled as the Mate ran past. "We've got two men overboard on the port side, and we're pulling away from them."

"I know, I know, I'm heading for the wheel-house now!" Cash delivered the words over his shoulder, never slowing his pace.

Josh followed, entering the bridge right behind Cash. Fingers of flame danced into the room from the blazing chart room. Smoke hung heavy in the air. Small fires of burning paper crackled everywhere. Cash grabbed the big brass handle of the engine-room telegraph and signaled "Full Ahead."

Josh snatched a portable fire extinguisher off the wall. He worked quickly, snuffing out the small fires burning all around them. Both men bent low and covered their noses with handkerchiefs, trying to keep the smoke out of their lungs. But it wasn't enough to stifle the cutting bite of burning marine paint and plywood on their air passages.

"I'll let her go Full Ahead," Cash said between coughs, "for about a minute or so to stop the ship." He coughed again. "I'm going out on the wing . . . can't breathe." He stumbled out the same door he'd entered.

Josh, satisfied he'd doused all the serious flames, and now coughing uncontrollably himself, quickly followed Cash. Both men stood on the wing, bent over, hands on their knees, while they took in the much needed clean air. Neither tried to speak until their coughing had partially subsided. When they seemed to have their breathing somewhat back to normal, they peered over the rail, looking for the men who'd been blown overboard with the explosion.

Both were in the water, pulling the life raft behind them as a shield. They were now swimming some 30 yards from the bow of the ship. Sniper fire splashed all around the two sailors. They held the raft in close to their heads, keeping it between them and the Japs. They'd smartly not dared to climb inside, exposing their whole bodies to the marksmen on shore.

The big engines had brought the ship to a halt. She now moved slightly forward. Cash charged into the wheel-house and flipped the engine-room telegraph to Stop Engines. He returned to where Josh, bent over, had started another coughing jag, trying to clear the smoke from his lungs. Smoke-induced tears streamed down the Second Mate's face. He struggled to get the cough under control.

Josh and Cash once again peered over the rail. The two men in the water were heading toward the bow, swimming along and pulling the life raft behind them.

"Josh, have you seen the Captain?" Cash's brows came together.

"Yeah. I didn't get a chance to tell you before. The Captain's on the rear bridge deck, unconscious. Sparks is with him." He coughed twice. "I didn't have time to find out what happened, or how he got there." Josh started down the ladder. "I'm going back now. See if I can help him."

Cash yelled after the departing figure. "After you get an update, get your butt back here. I want you on the bridge."

Josh waved his hand in acknowledgment.

Seaman Rork, on his way to the bridge to take the wheel, passed the Second Mate at the base of the ladder. Before he'd made the first step up, Cash saw him and gave him new orders. "Hold it, Rork. I'll take the wheel. You go back down, grab a couple of crewmen, and haul the Jacob's ladder to the bow. Then lower it for the two men who went overboard. They're getting close to the ship now." He took a quick look at the swimming sailors, then turned back to Rork. "When you get them on board, let me know immediately so we can get out of here." He paused, his eyes narrowed in thought. "In case you didn't know, the ship's phone system is dead. Call up to the forward three-inch gun tub. Have them get the message to Lieutenant Wagner through their communication setup. He'll let me know so I can get the engine going again. After that, I'll need you up here on the wheel. If you're busy, send me someone else . . . but get me a helmsman!"

Rork, waving his right arm in the air, yelled "Gotcha, Mate!" as he sprinted down the boat deck, jumping over burning chunks of debris.

Josh scurried down the deck on his way to check on the Captain. As he ran by, the condition of the one remaining lifeboat hit him. The pilot's strafing had left a number of holes in the lifeboat's metal hull. The

30-caliber holes could be patched easily enough, but the two hits by a 20mm had ripped openings six to ten inches across. If they had to abandon ship, the boat wouldn't do them any good, and it was the last lifeboat they had.

He climbed the ladder to the bridge after deck. He could see that the Captain still appeared unconscious. He asked Sparks if there had been any change."

"Not even a twitch. I'll stay here with him. The smoke in the radio shack is impossible to work in."

Josh advised Sparks to get Doc or Elijah to take a look at the Captain if he didn't come to in five minutes or so. Then Josh turned toward the doorway where his firefighters were alternating 30-second shifts on the hose. One man staggered out, frantically dragging in air and wiping the tears from his smoke-filled eyes. Are you making any progress in there?" Josh asked.

"Yeah . . . it won't be long now."

Josh went back to the bridge.

The mortar teams on the shore were soon silenced. Lieutenant Wagner nodded his head in satisfaction.

Realizing his lack of mobility in the gun tub, he returned down the ladder to the port bridge wing and reconnected his phone system. "OK, you guys," he yelled into the mike, "keep pouring that ammo into those mortar locations. I'll watch the Betty. He apparently hasn't made up his mind if he wants to try his luck against us without the Zero as his cover. Let's hope he thinks we're done for with all the smoke and fire the Kamikaze caused." The words "smoke" and "fire" gave birth to an idea in the Lieutenant's head. He turned it over in his mind. The more he thought about it, the better it sounded. Why not add to the smoke?

We could get the engine room to blow their tubes. (An expression used when they clean the smokestack periodically, causing soot and smoke to bellow out of the stack in a thick, black, dirty cloud.) That might really make the Betty think we're in deep trouble. He stepped back into the smoky wheel-house and called to Cash. "See if the engine room would blow the tubes right now. I mean really clean them out. I think it might convince the bomber pilot he could forget about us as his target; make him believe his Kamikaze friend has done his job for him. If we can make him think we've had an explosion, with an uncontrollable fire in the engine room, he'll most likely leave us alone."

"Sounds like a good plan." Cash headed for the voice tube. "And I'll have him jack up the fuel injection, and throttle back the forced draft blowers — that'll really fill the sky with gunk and smoke!"

Lieutenant Wagner returned to the badly damaged starboard bridge wing, standing precariously in the smoking rubble of what was left. The Merchant Marine volunteer in tub number six, some 30 feet from where Wagner stood yelled, "Hey, Lieutenant — we got no gunner on this twenty millimeter. Clark took Perry down to the infirmary to get some nasty burns taken care of. I'm one of the standby loaders. I don't know how to work this sucker."

Wagner looked up at the man who'd just given him this bad news. "Stay where you are. I'll get you a gunner." Unable to look into the number four gun tub right over his head because the ladder and platform had been blown away, he yelled, "Martinez! Can you send Hathaway over to man the twenty in tub number six? I'll get a seaman to load for you."

A voice from above answered, "This *is* Hathaway, Sir. Martinez was strapped into the gun, just like Perry in number six. He couldn't duck the fireball like I did. He caught some nasty burns, too. Clark took the two of them to the infirmary. I'm strapped into the gun, Sir, but I don't have a loader either, and I'll need a reload damn soon."

Chapter 15

LIEUTENANT WAGNER heaved a big sigh. Things could be a lot worse, but he couldn't help wonder what other problems he would have to face? Well, one thing at a time.

He spoke into the phone system, his voice steady. "I want one of you loaders on guns five or seven to take the gunner's spot on number six. There's a merchant seaman loader already there, but no gunner."

Cramer, in number seven, replied first. "I'm on my way, Lieutenant. You'll have to get a loader up here on seven to fill my spot."

"OK. I'll have a volunteer seaman up soon. Make sure Connelly has a full magazine before you leave." Wagner took a deep breath so his voice would carry, then cupped his hands around his mouth and yelled to the seaman. "Cramer's coming over from number seven to be your shooter. Hang in there!"

Moving quickly into the wheel-house, Wagner confronted Cash. "I need two of those volunteer loaders, one for tub seven and one for number four. Can do?"

"Oh, crap! I'm the only man on the bridge, and I'm waiting for news on those two who were blown overboard. As soon as they're brought on board I intend to get our butts out of here."

Both Wagner and Cash turned their heads when Josh entered from the port-side wing. They could hardly see him through the cloud of smoke that still hung in the room.

"Wow, what a mess!" The Second Mate shook his head. "What a mess!"

Cash sent Josh below to find two of the men on the list he removed from his pocket. "They're probably working fire hoses somewhere. Get any two and send them up to guns four and seven on the flying bridge. They volunteered as loaders, and we need them topside ASAP."

Josh didn't even come to a complete stop. He grabbed the list from Cash and took off down the port-side ladder.

Lieutenant Wagner, back out on the shaky, damaged starboard wing, watched the bomber circle, wondering how he could discourage the big plane from attacking.

"Williams," he called on his phone line, "reset a couple more shells for long-shot explosions . . . I mean real long. I don't want that Jap to get any ideas about making another run at us. Be sure to make the shots less than ten seconds apart. I want him to know he'd better keep his distance." He paused. "The rest of you still on this party line, concentrate on the beach. The crew on the aft big gun and I will watch out for the Betty."

The sky suddenly became hazy, then the sun all but disappeared. A black cloud of soot, smoke, and gunk belched out of the smokestack. The wind swirled. The midship became engulfed in the dark fog; it's pea-sized soot balls dancing across the decks everywhere. Wagner smiled. He spoke into his mike again to reassure his crew. "Don't let the smoke worry you, boys. It's just the engine room helping us to convince the Betty out there that we're done for."

As the thick smoke billowed out of the stack, it became apparent to Wagner that the gun tubs, all four of them at midship, could no longer see the beach and the puffs of smoke from the mortars. In fact, he couldn't see the bomber, the soot was so thick. "Williams," he shouted into the phone system, "keep everyone posted on the movements of the Betty. I have to find another observation location free from all this soot."

"Aye, Sir."

The team on the aft big gun let the first of the two long shots go that Wagner had ordered, followed quickly by another. The second shell exploded within 60 to 100 yards of the aircraft. The Betty immediately veered sharply to its left and headed south to get out of range of the *Albert A.*'s long gun.

Williams, more than pleased with his second shot, casually commented over the phone system, "Oh, Mr. Mitsubishi, did you wet your pants on that one?"

Laughter could be heard coming from several of the gun tubs.

As Lieutenant Wagner had anticipated, with the dense smoke from the ship's tubes, the enemy on shore seemed to think the Liberty ship had developed a more serious problem, and they commenced a new series of mortar launches. The ship now drifted about 50 yards farther away from shore than when the first attack had been made. Most of the enemy shells missed their target; but not all. One hit squarely on the hatch cover of the number four hold. Splinters of burning wood from hatch boards went flying everywhere, as did many of the intact three-by-five foot boards. Burning debris fell into the uncovered hold and onto the cargo stored there.

Wagner had restationed himself on the port-side bridge wing where the breeze had cleared the air of the dense, black sooty smoke belching from the smokestack. His gunner in tub eight called into the phone system, "I see smoke, Lieutenant. I think we've got a fire in number four hold."

Oh, God, what now? he thought. Hunched over, Lieutenant Wagner entered the wheel-house, looking for Cash. He spotted him on his knees, obviously trying to stay low enough to get some clean air. Fire extinguisher in one hand, the Mate crawled around putting out some small fires that had come alive again.

"What's your cargo in hold number four?" Wagner asked, then also dropped to his knees, so that he could breathe a little easier. "We have a fire reported down in the hold."

Cash removed the handkerchief over his nose. "Let me think a minute." The words squeaked out of his raw, irritated throat. "The manifest was in the chart room, so it's long gone." He slapped the handkerchief over his nose again and took a deep breath. "As I recall, they're earth-moving vehicles for the Seabees on the 'tween deck, and fifty-five gallon drums of diesel fuel on the lower deck."

Wagner coughed. "You better get a bunch of hoses going down there right away. If there are vehicles with gas in them, we're going to have a red-hot bulkhead against the munitions in number five."

After two more coughs Wagner rasped out, "Especially if it burns through the boards to the diesel fuel."

"Oh shit! You're right!" Cash jumped to his feet and ran to the doorway leading to what remained of the chart room and the Captain's quarters. From the companionway on the other side of the fire, he yelled to the three men alternately manning the fire hose and fighting the blaze. "We've got a fire in number four hold. Get all the hoses that'll reach there and start pouring water on it. That fire has top priority over all others. It has to be put out fast! Pass the word. Get as many men as you can muster."

"Did you guys hear me?"

"Loud and clear!" one of the seamen yelled back across the dense smoke and licking flames.

Cash, straining to get the message out, coughed with almost every word. "You guys break up so you can man all the hoses that'll reach that hold."

He couldn't wait for an answer. He needed some air. He raced for the bridge wing, gagging and coughing as he ran. He hoped the men had heard his last words over the noise the 20s made as they answered the launch of another mortar shell.

Five stories down, on the bottom deck of the engine room, Svenson, the Second Engineer, and Crosby, the First Engineer, attempted to get the Chief into a sitting position. He'd been placid enough while they had tried to stem the flow of blood from a cut on his head. They hadn't been able to completely stop it, but they'd at least slowed it down some. Now they wanted to get him to the infirmary, but he wasn't making it easy.

"Yeesus *Christ*, can't you just let me lay here?" He flailed his arms to push away their hands.

"No, damn it! We've been hit, and hit bad. For all we know, we may have to abandon ship momentarily. If that word comes down, it's not the time to decide you need to go topside." Svenson, good friend that he was, glared into the Chief's eyes. "Besides, you need to get where Doc can take a look at you . . . don't argue. You're going up now — and that's final."

Feeling sorry for the grizzled old Engineer, Crosby took a softer tone. He could see the man's right knee, already turning blue, had been injured. "If we get you on your feet, Chief, you think you can support your weight on your good leg?"

"Yeesus *Christ*, you two screw-knuckles don't understand," he drew in a shaky breath. "I broke my friggin' leg!" He waved their hands away again. "Now, vill you leave me alone." He laid back down on the iron deck.

"That does it!" Svenson snorted. He turned to Crosby. "I'm going to take him up piggy-back style." He faced the Chief, his expression clearly determined. "You old buzzard, you're going to have to hang on to my neck. I'll need my hands and arms to get us up to the main deck." He pointed at the four narrow ladders they'd have to climb. "I won't be able to hang on to you while I climb up those friggin' things."

"What do you want me to do?" Crosby looked worried. "How can I help?"

Svenson, his lips in a tight line, drew in a deep breath. "Follow close behind me. You'll probably have to give this cantankerous old fart the wedgie of his life."

Crosby's eyebrows shot up. "What do you mean?"

"That arm looks to be injured." Svenson pointed to the Chief's twisted left arm. "He won't be able to hold much of his body weight. You grab a handful of his pants from behind and, best as you can, lift as much of his weight as possible."

Crosby pursed his lips, took in a deep breath, then let it out in an almost whistle. He licked his lower lip. "Let's hope nothing hits the ship while we're going up those damn, oil-slick ladders. If it does, there's likely to be three casualties laying down here at the bottom."

"Oh, Yeesus *Christ*, dis von't vork. You'll slip and kill us all!" the Chief bellowed.

"Pipe down, you old Scandihoovian reprobate, just hang on for the wedgie ride of your life."

Through much moaning and groaning, swearing and blustering, the two men finally got the Chief on Svenson's back. The old man wrapped his good arm around Svenson's neck and let his legs hang straight down. The three made their way to the first ladder.

Svenson grabbed the two rails, took a deep breath, and mumbled, "Hang on, Chief. Your horse is ready to gallop."

"Giddi-oop!" the Chief said through clenched teeth.

As Svenson put his foot on the first step, Crosby looked back at the Third Engineer. "You're in charge, Gallagher. We'll be back as soon as possible."

He grabbed the Chief's beltless pants from behind and lifted most of the old-timer's weight. He climbed the ladder close behind Svenson, one hand on the rail, the other clutching the slack of the Chief's khakis.

"Yeesus *Christ* . . . you're squashing my balls, Crosby."

Crosby tried to make light of the situation. "See, Chief, with our help your leg doesn't hurt as much anymore, does it?"

"Ooohhh," moaned the Chief, "vurra, vurra funny Mr. Crosby . . . Ooohhh, you're neutering me . . . I'll never be a man again." His arm tightened on Svenson's neck. "Vill you stop . . . pleeeeeze?"

Svenson paused on the second landing, not only to get his breath, but to get the Chief to relax the hold he had on the Engineer's neck. If it got any tighter, Svenson just might black out from lack of air.

Crosby loosened his grip on the Chief's pants. "OK, Chief, rearrange your family jewels as best you can. We'll have to continue the same wedgie fashion the rest of the way up."

The Chief, standing on his one good leg, sighed with relief at the brief respite. "Ooohh, dat's better . . . ah, yes, mooch better."

Crosby grinned. "OK, Svenson, let's get this show on the road." He grabbed the Chief's pants again, dragging a sharp breath from the old man. "Infirmary, here we come," he announced as they started up the next ladder.

With another dull *thunk*, a direct mortar hit again, this time on the forward starboard side, on the eight-man liferaft. It disintegrated, along with its launcher platform, throwing small pieces of burning, smoldering wood and canvas in every direction.

"Son of a bitch!" Rork brushed the burning piece of canvas from his forearm.

He and the two seamen he'd recruited had rolled out the Jacob's ladder and were dragging it up the port side of the ship, crab-style, when the last mortar hit. They briefly paused in their journey when the ship shook with the impact of the mortar shell. The smoldering debris rained down on them, but Rork had been the only one to get slightly burned.

Back to work, he thought, ignoring the hot, red spot on his arm. "OK, guys. Let's pull in unison." He'd placed the two men on one side, and he took the other. "Heave . . . heave . . . heave. That's it. We're almost there."

They lifted the ladder and dropped the end over the bow. Foot by foot, they lowered it over the railing, anchoring it when the lead end touched the water.

The two sailors who'd been blown overboard had been smart enough to stay low in the water until the ladder dangled in place. Even so, sniper fire sent water spurting up into the air around them every time the waves brought their faces high enough to be seen on shore.

Seeing that the sniper fire was concentrating on the two men, Rork yelled up to the gunner's mate on the forward big gun. "Palmer, ask your Lieutenant to lay down some sort of cover fire to make those snipers hunker down long enough to get two of our men back on board. They're hanging on the Jacob's ladder now."

Within a minute the 20s laid down a two-minute barrage on the beach where the snipers had taken up positions. Smoke, fire, and flying debris erupted from areas of the jungle most likely inhabited by the shooters. The 20s did their job. Only a few shots were fired at the two men as they clambered up the Jacob's ladder to safety.

Rork helped the first man up over the rail. A short, stocky guy, he rolled over the railing with a grin. "Now, that's what I call a cool and refreshing swim."

The men couldn't help but laugh, the merriment increasing when the second man climbed over, raised his arms in a victory gesture, spread his feet, and yelled, "Ta-da!" The whine of a sniper's bullet past his head brought his arms and body down quickly.

Rork called again. "Hey, Palmer. Tell the Lieutenant thanks for the cover. Will you also tell him to let the Mate in the wheel-house know we've got the men safely aboard. Now he can get us out of here." Turning to the seamen, he said, "Let's hurry and get this ladder back on board." He pointed to one of them. "Olson, the Mate's going to need you on the wheel. Better get going."

The three men who'd been taking turns manning the hose and attempting to control the fire in and around the Captain's quarters ran past Sparks where he sat watchfully observing the unconscious Captain. They dragged 50 feet of hose behind them. Sparks had heard the Mate's orders and knew they were heading for the fire in hold number four. Not knowing what the cargo might be, he didn't want to think about what might happen if they couldn't get the fire under control in the hold next to the ammo.

He could hear the men yelling to each other as the teams assembled to man the hoses. Ignoring the latest mortar hit up forward, they stayed their positions, their first priority being the fire in number four. Fortunately for all concerned, the hold, positioned in back of the midship housing, was a safe location from sniper fire. It also enabled the men to fight the fire from above, shooting water down from the main deck.

Sparks knelt next to the prone man. "Captain, are you coming out of it yet?"

The Captain's eyes fluttered.

"Come on, Captain, wake up. We need you on the bridge." Maybe the thought of duty and responsibility might get through the darkness of the Captain's injury, whatever it might be, Sparks reasoned. No further response came from Captain Daly. Sparks shook his head in frustration. What could he do? He gently ran his fingers over the monstrous lump on the Captain's forehead, and noted the bleeding from the split skin had almost subsided. Since he'd received the damage to his head when he'd crashed into the bulkhead, a new question came to mind. Quite possibly, that blow could have done more than just knock the Captain unconscious. Maybe a concussion? Hopefully, not a neck injury. Whatever it might be, the man needed some special attention.

Sparks hesitated for only a moment. He hated to leave the Captain alone, but he had to get some help. He took off on a run, heading for the makeshift hospital in the officer's mess. He came to a halt in the doorway. All hell had broken loose. He gazed in amazement.

Crosby and Svenson had staggered into the room just ahead of him, carrying the injured Chief. The two cuts on his face and head made a red trail down the side of his face. One arm hung loosely at his side, and from the looks of his right knee, now swollen to the size of a football, he wouldn't be walking on that leg any time soon.

Cookie sat on a bench. The very hot, bully beef borscht, that had spilled over his bare legs, had left them scorched. The upper thigh on his left leg looked an ugly dark reddish-purple. Raul sat next to him, holding a hand on which blisters had already raised. Men who had been too close to the fire ball following the Kamikaze hit had been brought in right after the crash. The most severely injured had been Martinez and Perry, the gunners in tubs four and six. Each occupied a mattress on the floor of the infirmary. Their burns already had been attended to with salves and sterile gauze. As the medics continued to treat other victims, they watched out of the corners of their eyes for any indication the gunners might be going into shock.

Doc and Elijah worked as rapidly as they could, flitting from one man to the next. Sparks hurried over to Doc. "The Captain's hurt. He needs help." He shook Doc's arm, trying to make the Purser look at him.

Doc never looked up, but continued to apply a butterfly bandage to a deep, ugly cut over the eye of one of the seamen. "Well, so do these people. How serious is it?"

Sparks hurriedly told the story, stressing the fact the Captain had been unconscious for quite awhile — at least it seemed that way to Sparks.

Elijah, the more experienced of the two medics, had heard the conversation. "Is there a stateroom on that deck that hasn't suffered fire damage?"

Sparks nodded. "Only the gunnery officer's. Why?"

Elijah pursed his lips. "I don't think the Cap'n should be moved. I'll come with you. We'll take the mattress out of the lieutenant's room and carefully bed the Cap'n down on the deck where you have him now. After he comes to, we can learn how serious his head injury is."

Elijah, who'd been kneeling while applying salve to a badly burned leg, then wrapping it in gauze, stood arching his back. With his hands over his head, he stretched his big, black frame toward the ceiling, then spread a hand out in front of him, pointing. "OK, Sparks, lead the way."

The two jogged off, Sparks in the lead, making their way to Wagner's quarters. Lieutenant Wagner would have to go without his mattress — not that anyone would have time to sleep in the near future.

Chapter 16

SPARKS SCRAMBLED UP the inside ladder toward the bridge deck and pointed at the head of the stairs. "That's his room dead ahead. Mine's the one next to it." When they reached the opening to Spark's room, he said, "You can see what happened to my bed and mattress . . . nothing left but charcoal."

Elijah stuck his head through the doorway. "You're right. It's a mess. The guys who put the fire out really soaked everything in the room: your bunk, your papers, what's left of your clothes." A softness came into his eyes when he turned toward Sparks. "Even the Bible on your desk got wet." Elijah rubbed a big hand across his short hair. "You think maybe I could borrow it for a little while? I gave mine to Don Lind when he got that fungus infection in his ears down in Hollandia and almost went crazy. You remember?"

Sparks nodded. "Yeah. It was so bad they had to ship him home."

Elijah shook his head. "Poor guy. It seemed like he needed the comfort of the Word more than I did at the time. I sure do miss having my Bible, though."

"You can have mine for as long as you want, Elijah. In fact, keep it. I have another one at home."

Elijah's eyes glistened as he tenderly lifted the Book and shoved it into his pants next to his belly. "Thanks, Sparks. Now, let's get that mattress, and get out of this smoke."

Together they heaved Wagner's mattress off his bunk and wrestled it to the rear bridge deck, plopping it down next to the still unconscious Captain.

Elijah knelt next to the prone figure. "How did he get out here?" He ran his fingers over the bulging, blue goose-egg on the man's forehead, being careful not to reopen the cut.

"I pulled him out of the radio shack by his ankles after I'd put out the smoldering spots on his clothes and hair. It was the only way I could get him away from the smoke."

"This is a mighty big bump. The move could've injured his neck or spine." He looked up at Sparks. "I guess any damage that might happen by moving him's already been done."

Sparks felt his stomach knot up. What if the Captain was paralyzed? What if, because of the way he'd dragged the Skipper, some brain damage had occurred? Sparks shook his head. What else could he have done though?

His concerns must have shown on his face, because Elijah said, "You did what you had to do, Sparks. If you'da left him in the smoke-filled room he'd be dead by now."

He ran his hands over the injured man, feeling for any broken bones, then checked his vital signs. "I don't see nothin' wrong with him. Guess we'll just have to wait for him to wake up to find out if he's OK." He looked around the deck. "This seems like a fairly safe place. Let's get him on the mattress and cover him up. I don't think we should move him any more."

Elijah pushed himself up from his kneeling position. "I'll take his head, you take his feet." He slid his hands under the Captain's shoulders, wedging the man's head between his forearms. "Move him on three. One . . . two . . . three . . ."

Together, they slid Captain Daly onto the mattress and covered him with a dry blanket they'd found in Wagner's room. "I'd better get back to help'n Doc. You keep an eye on the Cap'n and let us know when he wakes up."

"Will do . . . and thanks for your help."

Elijah pulled the Bible from his pants and gestured with it. "No, thank *you*, Sparks."

Sparks watched the big man sprint away. A man of many talents, he thought — baker, cook, medic, and the closest thing to a chaplain the men had seen on any merchant ship.

Meanwhile, not knowing what the Jap bomber's intentions were, Lieutenant Wagner continuously kept his eye on the Betty, which now moved well out of range of the *Albert A.*'s big guns. He lowered his binoculars. Carefully, he took several more steps out on the rickety remainder of the starboard bridge wing. By flexing his knees as if he were readying himself to jump, he could feel the deck move erratically under his feet. Twisted metal and two ladders that were hanging on by a single weld swung with the motion of the ship. One glance to his right revealed the severity of the Kamikaze hit. Not much remained of the chart room and Captain's quarters.

Some smoke still billowed upward, not only from the damage on this deck, but also from what used to be the overhead of the Second and Third Mates' quarters one deck below. The ceilings of those two rooms had been peeled back on the Zero's impact; the embers still smoldered. Wagner shook his head as he looked around. It could have been so much worse.

Again raising his field glasses, a smile crept onto his face. Turning on his all-call, he announced to his men, "You guys can relax, at least for now." He watched the plane through his binoculars as it soared out of sight. "The Betty's heading northeasterly towards the airfield and home. I guess the Japanese crew took the bait. When the engine room blew the tubes and all that black smoke covered the ship, they must have concluded a catastrophic explosion had taken place and we were dead in the water." He lowered his field glasses, letting them hang against his chest.

The *thunk* of new mortar fire from the beach reached their ears.

"OK, you guys, get after those mortar launchers. Let's see if we can't shut them up for good."

The gunners on the 20s let forth with a vicious, teeth-chattering barrage, once again silencing the enemy fire coming from the beach . . . at least temporarily. But the silence didn't stop the Armed Guard crew from perusing the beach, searching for any action, still intent on catching any puffs of smoke from a mortar launch, should there be one.

Wagner took this quiet time to ascertain the condition of his troops. "OK, men, time to report in. Other than the burns suffered by Martinez and Perry, did we suffer any other casualties out there?"

"Yes, Sir. This is Franklin, tub number two. At one of the Zero's passes, thirty caliber shells ricocheted around in the tub like mad. Morgan has two wounds. They're not life-threatening, Sir, but he *is* bleeding."

"Will he need help getting to sick bay?"

"No, Sir."

"When he goes, you're gonna need a loader?"

"Yes, Sir. But Palmer said Douglas could come over from the forward three-incher if I need him."

Wagner attempted to clear his throat, still dry and scratchy from all the smoke he'd dealt with since the Kamikaze hit. "Palmer, did you hear that? Can you release Douglas to serve as a loader for Franklin until I can find a merchant seaman not tied up with fighting fires?"

"Yes, Sir. He's on his way."

"And Franklin, send Morgan to the infirmary. Be sure to remind him to hunker down and hug the rail. Don't want a sniper putting a third hole in him." He paused. "Any others?"

Williams cut in. "We got one back aft on the three-incher. Crenshaw caught a bullet in the foot. We've stopped the bleeding for the moment, but there are broken bones involved. It's serious and he needs help, but we won't take him down to the infirmary until we get a little farther from shore. Where our ladder down is located would make us too big a target for the snipers. It'll take two of us to carry him. Is that OK?"

"Yes — of course." With the back of his index finger Wagner squeezed the sweat from under his helmet. "If there are no other injuries . . ."

Roberts, on number nine gun broke in. "Ackman took a nick in the butt from a ricocheting bullet. It's about as serious as a nosebleed, but he wants to take home a purple heart. Is it OK if I send him to the infirmary?"

That brought a laugh from Lieutenant Wagner, and several others on the party-line. "Why not? You guys all deserve a medal for the fight you just put up." He took a quick breath. "Unfortunately, it's not over yet. Roberts, when Ackman goes, you'll need a loader, too."

"Yes, Sir. But Ackman just put a new cartridge in for me. I'm fully loaded and ready."

"That's good. You guys on the aft big gun, when you've taken Crenshaw down to the infirmary, one of you report to tub nine to act as a loader for Roberts if I haven't gotten a seaman up there to take over the job. Is everyone else OK?"

He bowed his head when he heard the chorus of affirmative answers, then, with eyes closed, offered up a quick "Thank you, Lord. Thank you for watching over my boys."

"If there are no other injuries to report, I want all of you to stay alert in your tubs. Keep pounding those mortar installations until we're out of their range. That's your number-one priority for the moment, but keep your eyes peeled for any enemy aircraft that might try to sneak up and take another whack at destroying us. We don't want any more Kamikazes going to their promised land a big hero at our expense."

A chorus of "Amens" and "Yes Sirs" sounded from the crews.

Sparks once more tried to rouse the Captain, but got no response. There seemed to be nothing more he could do for the man but keep him comfortable — at least not until the Skipper regained consciousness. Since it seemed comparatively safe to leave him, Sparks decided to check on the radio shack, just a short distance away.

Smoke still hung heavy in the companionway. The door to the shack was closed. How unusual, he thought. He gingerly opened the door and slipped inside, pleased to find the air relatively free of smoke. He quickly closed it behind him. Junior labored in the corner over the broken typewriter table, trying to get it to stand up on its remaining three legs.

"Hey, Junior, glad to see you're all right!" He grinned. "You were smart to close this door and put a scoop in the porthole. The air is ten times better in here than in the companionway."

"Yeah. I guess the door will stay that way as long as the fire is still smoldering in the Captain's quarters . . . or should I say what used to be the Captain's rooms and the chart room. Where they were is just a big crater in the side of the ship." He continued to try to wedge the typewriter table between the transmitter and the bulkhead. "How'd this table get pulled loose from the floor bolts? Were you in here when it happened?"

Sparks laughed. "I was typing in the three-minute 'silent' period into the log when I heard Wagner yell, *He's going to hit us*! I didn't know what he was yelling about; then a force like a speeding Mack truck hit me from behind. The next thing I knew I was wrapped up on top of the overturned typewriter table in a ball of fire." He shuddered at the memory. "If we make it through today, I should have some nasty bruises to show you tomorrow."

Junior took a good look at Sparks. His lips twitched. He wanted to laugh, but held it in, realizing the seriousness of Sparks' appearance. "Look at you! You've got no eyebrows; your hair is almost gone. It's even shorter than the 'butch' cut the Captain gave you. Your whole head and face looks sunburned. Does it hurt?"

"Not too much. You remember the burn we got in Sansapor, when we went seashell hunting balls-ass naked and ended up with two big water blisters on the cheeks of our untanned butts?"

Junior nodded. "Yeah. We had to stand up to eat and do our watch."

"Well, it feels like that."

The two men looked at each other. The throbbing of the big, three-cylinder engine caught their attention when the ship shuddered. They could feel the ship moving, sliding backwards in the water, away from the island.

"I guess the men who'd been blown overboard are now safe on the ship, or else we wouldn't be moving. Let's get this place in some sort of working order." Sparks swept the charred and wet pieces of paper off the work area of the console with the flat of his forearm. "See if you can find something to tie down the table to the radiator. We've got the four o'clock BAMS coming in, in seventeen minutes. I've got to see if the equipment is still working."

"OK, I'm off to find us some rope."

Sparks snapped his fingers to get Junior's attention. "Maybe you'd better stay here for a couple of minutes more while I go check on the Captain. I want to see if he's regained consciousness yet. I'll be right back."

When Sparks returned to the rear deck, Captain Daly was sitting up, rubbing his head, a silly grin on his face. He looked confused. "What the hell? How did I get here, Sparks?"

"I dragged you out here, Captain. Sorry I couldn't carry you, but —" Sparks put his finger to the Captain's cheek. "I guess I'm responsible for the cherry scruff mark. You were face down when I pulled you from the radio shack out to here." He knelt down to take a closer look at the raw, bruised cheek. "When the Kamikaze hit, you were blown into the radio shack by a fire ball. I mean that literally. You came hurtling through the door as if you were making a flying tackle on someone. You hit the bulkhead with your noggin. You've been out ever since." He studied the Captain's eyes. "Do you remember any of that?"

Captain Daly shook his head slowly from side to side.

Sparks stood up. "How's your neck and head? Are you feeling OK?"

The Captain rubbed the back of his neck. "I'll survive. How's the ship?" He paused, his expression worried. "Did that crazy Kamikaze kill any of the men?"

"I don't know, Sir. It's possible, but I haven't heard of any fatalities. I was down in the infirmary a short time ago and nobody mentioned any deaths then." He shoved his hands into his back pockets. "There are a number of injuries. Doc and Elijah are taking care of them."

"What else happened while I've been napping?" He closed his eyes tightly and shook his head, obviously trying to clear away the remaining cobwebs.

"I understand there's been a lot of damage, but none serious enough to stop us now that we're free from the rocks."

"Who's in charge on the bridge?" The Captain struggled to reach up to the top of the rail with his right arm, finally aiding it with his left.

"I keep hearing the Mate's voice barking out orders, Sir."

The Captain attempted to get to his feet. "I gotta get up there." He fell back on one knee, then plopped hard on his butt. He sucked in a quick breath through clenched teeth, sounding like a fresh can of coffee, when the vacuum seal is broken. "Wow . . . am I dizzy." His right arm slid from the rail and dangled by his side.

Sparks hurried to help prop him up against the rail. "You better stay put until Doc or Elijah can look you over. You took a mighty big clout on your head . . . and look at your arms. You've got some bad burns that need dressing, and the cut on your head needs sewing up. You just sit tight and I'll get someone to take care of you."

The Captain held up his hand. "Before you go, your quarters are right there and I have an elephant-sized headache. Will you get me some aspirin — if you have any?"

Sparks nodded. "Be right back." Seven steps took him to his room. He reached for the hinged mirror door to the medicine cabinet. In the reflection he saw what had made Junior laugh. He placed the back of his hand against his cheek, feeling the heat radiating from it. "Man, that's a sunburn and a half," he muttered. He opened the cabinet and grabbed the aspirin bottle, then filled a glass with water. Hurrying back to the Captain's side, he put both into the man's hand. "Here you go."

He shook three white pills into his hand.

Sparks started to go, then hesitated. A big grin crept onto his face. "I can't wait until you take a look in the mirror, Sir. You thought I gave you a bad haircut. Wait 'til you see what the Jap did."

Captain Daly reached up with his left hand and rubbed his crusty, burned hair. It crumbled and fell into his lap. Looking up, he caught Spark's attention and burst into laughter. "Is there any left, or am I completely bald?"

Chapter 17

STILL LAUGHING, Sparks headed for the infirmary. At the head of the stairs he yelled, "I'll be back in time for the BAMS schedule, Junior. Gotta take care of the Captain first."

"Take your time," Junior replied. "If we got a coded message, we couldn't decipher it anyway. The code books went up in smoke with the chart room."

Sparks mulled over the problem Junior had just brought to light as he scooted down the two flights. If we should get a message, we'll have to figure a way to work around that, he thought. First things first, though. Let's get the Captain taken care of.

He paused in the doorway of the mess hall. One of the gunners had just arrived. Elijah worked over him delicately with a pair of tweezers while Hogan held a flashlight on the injured man's eye. The Navy

man had caught a small fragment of brass from a 20mm shell, spit out of the breech of the gun he manned. It had imbedded itself in his eye. Elijah, concentrating on the task, was taking great care to remove it.

Doc finished applying the salve and wrappings to a burn victim he was working on. He stood and stretched, trying to relieve his cramped muscles.

Sparks rushed to his side. "Doc, Elijah's busy and the Captain's awake. He needs your help. He's got some serious burns, and a bad cut on his scalp."

"Good timing. We seem to have things under control down here, for the time being. Let's go take care of him." Doc scooped up burn salve, tape, and several rolls of gauze.

As they made their way up the two ladders to the place where the Captain waited, Sparks filled in the medic on the Captain's condition and his attempt to stand.

Doc listened intently while he lit a cigarette and took a deep drag. "Oh, I needed this. I've been so busy I haven't even had time to light up."

They stepped out onto the rear bridge deck. Looking at the Captain, Doc shook his head, his cigarette perched in its usual spot in the center of his mouth. "By golly, you're right Sparks. He does have a rather unusual hair style." The cigarette, as usual, flapped wildly up and down as he talked. "When I finish putting on this salve and get him bandaged, he's going to look just darling."

Captain Daly glared at his Purser turned medic. "Don't get cute, Doc, just get me bandaged up and then help me to the bridge."

Doc laughed. "We'll see about that. You might have to rest for a bit."

Captain Daly's eyes narrowed. "I'll be the judge of that."

Doc knelt over the Captain as he applied several butterfly tapes to pull together the split skin on the Captain's head. "Now, let's take care of those burns."

Sparks grinned. "I wish I could stay and help, but I've gotta catch a BAMS schedule in three minutes, and I'm not even sure my receiver is working." He turned to leave. "He's all yours, Doc."

The voice of the Mate, the speaking trumpet to his mouth, boomed first forward, then aft, from the port-side bridge wing. "Someone find Boats. I want him to get a crew working on rigging those booms for open water. And I need Chips to meet the Second Mate up at the fo'c'sle to heave in the anchor that's left. It's still dangling over the side. Then, Lingayen Gulf . . . here we come."

Ivan walked into the bridge from the smoke-filled housing entrance as Cash came in from the wing entrance. "Those are words I wasn't sure I'd ever hear, Cash." His smile spread across his face. "Now if we can clear the area before more Bettys find us, my heart may stop beating in double-time."

Cash nodded and cleared his raspy throat. "Guess what? I've got another job for you."

Ivan's eyebrows raised in question. "What?"

"Get some men and a lot of chain. I want you to strap down the load of landing plates so they won't slide over the side in heavy seas. We worked our butts off to save them for the Seabees. It would be a damn shame to lose them now."

The smile slowly disappeared from Ivan's face. "Geez, I forgot all about how precariously they're stacked. I'll get right on it."

Cash gave Ivan a thumbs-up as the Third Mate left the bridge, then put down the speaking trumpet. It seemed to him the ship was far enough off shore now to turn around. Under his orders, Harold Olson, the skinny, six-foot-five wheelman, swung the rudder hard to the starboard while the ship still moved full astern.

Cash moved to the engine room telegraph. He whipped the brass communicator into the Full Ahead position. The throbbing engine halted momentarily. The engine room signaled confirmation of the Full Ahead order. Moments later the big propeller again churned the water. The ship shuddered, then slowly moved forward.

The familiar vibration on his feet brought a smile to Cash's face. He whacked his wheelman on the back. "OK, let's get out of here, Olson." He pointed at the two shapes in the distance. "Those two ships bearing down on us are your target for the moment. Let's go!"

The gangly man swung the wheel hard to port. "Yes, Sir. I'm all for that!"

The *Albert A. Robinson* swung around and headed north, directly toward the two approaching vessels.

Lieutenant Wagner walked into the wheel-house. The smile on his face could almost be called a smirk. "I know we're not out of the woods yet, but I must confess, it sure feels good to be under our own power again." He stood by the thick bridge window and trained his binoculars on the oncoming craft. "Yep, they're ours. Two LSTs to the rescue . . . a little late, but a welcome sight anyway."

Cash pointed in the direction of the ships and laughed. "Lookee there. It's like they knew they were being talked about."

From one of the LSTs a signal light sent out "blip-blip, blip-blip, blip-blip," the call signal indicating they wanted to communicate via the big lights.

Wagner flipped on his phone system that reached all the gun emplacements. "Someone tell Flags he's needed on the flying bridge immediately to work the light. Those Navy ships want to talk to us." He turned to Cash. "I'll go up and see what they want. As soon as I find out I'll come back down and bring you up to date."

Cash nodded.

Wagner started out the starboard exit on the run toward the ladder leading to the flying bridge on the upper deck, as he normally did. He rounded the corner and almost stepped off into a one-deck drop.

He sucked in a breath. "Wow, that was close."

Still shaking his head, he quickly returned to the confines of the bridge. "We're going to have to rope off that area, Cash, before someone steps off into space . . . like I almost did."

Cash laughed. "You almost took the big step?"

"I sure did." Lieutenant Wagner felt the heat in his cheeks and knew he looked embarrassed. "Guess I'll have to go through the companionway and up from the rear bridge deck to get topside now."

Cash, still laughing at the gunnery officer's near header, agreed. "Yeah, we're all going to have to get used to that. Locking down the door to the destroyed area would be the easiest way, but then we couldn't get any cross ventilation." He shook his head. "No, your idea's best. I'll get it roped off right."

"What's that you're going to rope off, Cash?"

Both men turned at the sound of the familiar voice.

Captain Daly stepped into the wheel-house from the hazy companionway, almost bumping into Lieutenant Wagner on his way out.

Wagner huffed a laugh. "Could that be our good Captain Robert Daly, or is it the haunting Davy Jones, sheik of all ancient mariners?" He raised his eyebrows at the strips of gauze wound around the Captain's head.

"I think Doc got carried away when he patched up my burns and the cut on my head. You know Doc, always jokin' around. I haven't seen what I look like yet, but the way he chuckled while he wrapped it, I imagine I look rather odd."

The Captain patted his wrapped head. "I need to get brought up to date. Tell me, what's happening? What happened while I was out?"

Wagner pointed to the Mate. "Cash, you'll have to fill him in. I gotta get going. I have to meet with Flags." He gently patted Daly on the back. "It's sure good to see you on your feet again, Captain."

To avoid the lingering smoke in the companionway, he took a deep breath he could hold, then trotted off, past the radio shack to the rear bridge deck . . . then up the ladder to the flying bridge.

He reached the big light on the port side just seconds ahead of Flags. Shocked by the Signalman's appearance, he burst out with, "What the hell have you been doing? Where you been? You're soaking wet. You been standing in the shower to keep cool?"

Flags, a short, very muscular man, looked down at his dripping wet clothes and soggy shoes. "No, Sir. Brett and I were the ones blown over the side when the Jap came in. We were working on the signal light idea from behind the smokestack; trying to come up with a way to make the area bulletproof as you'd requested. When the strafing bullets from the Zero started whizzing by, we jumped into tub seven. It's right alongside the smokestack on the port side. When the Jap got hit and made his wide approach, we had no idea he intended to Kamikaze us. We watched as he came closer, figuring he'd go down any second. We wanted to see him hit the water."

"I'm sure we all assumed he'd dunk before he reached us."

"But he didn't. He just kept coming."

"That he did, but that still doesn't explain how you got in the water."

"When he was about a half mile out, Brett and I climbed up on the high step in the tub to watch. He wasn't firing and the gunners in the tub we were in couldn't fire without risking hitting the personnel in tub number six." Flags shrugged his shoulders, a silly grin on his face. "I guess it was stupid, but we never expected him to reach the ship."

"You used the right term . . . stupid." Wagner shook his head as if he couldn't believe anyone would do something so dumb. "But how did you get in the water?"

Flags hunched his shoulders again. "I don't know about Brett, but I was standing on my tiptoes on the step behind the gunner when the Zero nosed up and hit the bridge deck housing. I had no idea he had a bomb on board, or that the concussion from the blast would be so strong. I was flying ass-over-teakettle before I could blink my eyes. When I came up for air after hitting the water, there was Brett beside me, looking just as dumbfounded as I felt."

Wagner couldn't stop shaking his head in disbelief. "You two idiots are lucky to be alive." He had an afterthought. "Where's your life jacket?"

"Well, Sir, the Jap snipers saw us before anyone on the ship did. They started firing. Every wave brought us high in the water, and we heard the bullets go whizzing by. It didn't take us long to realize we'd be better off without the floaters. We dumped them so we could keep all but our faces under water."

"That at least was better thinking than what got you in the water in the first place. You made a wise choice. I suppose you have an equally plausible explanation for why you're not wearing a helmet."

"Yes Sir, I do. Did you ever try to swim fully clothed with one of those buckets on your head? They're a load and a half. We both dumped them before the two-man raft dropped our way. We swam like hell to get to it and used it as a shield."

The Lieutenant looked the dripping man over once again. "I repeat . . . you two are lucky to be alive. I see you brought a pad and pencil. I guess you're all right. Are you ready to work the light?"

"Sure." Flags made a quick gesture toward the big light. "Let's get to work. We don't have to worry about sniper fire this far out."

"First, let's see what they want, then I have a message for you to send to them."

Flags swung the big light around and aimed it at the oncoming ships. He flipped on the switch and quickly flashed the letters "K" and "GA" ("OK, go ahead)."

The light on one of the LSTs quickly flickered a message. As Flags scribbled it down on his scratch pad, Wagner read over his shoulder. "Do you still need our assistance?"

"Tell them we're free of the rocks, but we need their medical assistance."

Flags rapidly flipped the handle on the Venetian blind assembly of the signaling light, flashing the message to the approaching ship.

Moments later the answer came. "What is the nature of your injuries?"

Wagner, still looking over Flags's shoulder, nodded. "OK . . . tell them we have five men with bullet wounds, eight with burns, one with an eye injury, and one with a badly fractured knee." He paused a moment. "You'd better add . . . 'Can we transfer them to your sick bay for professional help? We have no doctors or trained medics on board.'"

The two ships were close enough now to see clearly with the naked eye that they were LSTs. Even their numbers were readable with the binoculars. The Signalman on LST 673, the ship they'd been communicating with, responded, "Proceed on your present course to Lingayen Gulf. We'll pull alongside and take your injured aboard with our body sling basket."

Wagner had gotten the answer he'd wanted. "That's good enough for me," he said to Flags. "Tell them, thanks, then you can sign off. I'll go tell the Captain what we're going to do."

Flags paused, looking at Wagner uncertainly, as if he had a question.

Wagner frowned. "What?"

"Shouldn't we tell them we have munitions on board in case more Jap planes find us and decide to bomb us, or we get hit with a torpedo? We'll be traveling within a hundred miles of several Japanese-controlled islands . . . and we're not that far from the Negros airfield."

Wagner grinned and winked. "We have men on board that need their professional medical help. I don't intend to give them any reason why they can't get close enough to take our injured aboard for the necessary treatment that we can't provide. Let's get them on the LST, then maybe I'll remember your question." Still grinning, he asked, "Understand?"

Flags nodded. "OK Sir, but those two Captains are not going to be happy when they hear about the situation later. In fact, I'd guess they're going to be damn mad when they find out if we'd taken a hit in the munitions hold while traveling with them, we'd probably have sunk them both."

The grin slowly disappeared from Wagner's face. His gaze narrowed, his nostrils flared. "Flags, we all have our personal moral standings and goals, our responsibilities in this war. My top personal priority is to bring back home the men under my command in as good a condition as I possibly can."

He dragged in a deep breath and let it seep out slowly. His words came out through clenched teeth, each one spoken firmly and distinctly. "I'll let them know so they can disburse to a safe distance once we get our casualties on board the LST . . . and not before."

Flags looked chagrined. "Sorry, Sir . . . I didn't mean to second-guess your intentions. I'll sign off with them now, but I think I'd better stay up here just in case they have more to say."

Glad he'd gotten through to the Signalman and made him understand the necessity of keeping their little secret for the time being, Lieutenant Wagner softened his tone. "Good idea, Flags." He patted the young man on the back. "You were right to remind me about the ammo. Remind me again, after . . . I repeat . . . after our men have been transferred." He smiled again. "I may take some heat for it, but what the hell. I've been in hot water with the big brass before."

Plodding along at ten knots, the SS *Albert A. Robinson* soon had LST 673 riding alongside with about 40 feet separating them. A line, strung between the two, carried the body baskets from one to the other. One by one the injured men took a ride from the damaged Liberty to the LST, where they could receive much-needed medical treatment.

Captain Daly, happy to be back in command of the ship, stood on the bridge wing and anxiously watched the process. It seemed to be taking place without any mishaps.

He looked at the big man standing next to him. "Damn it, I'm OK, Elijah." He patted the bandage on his head. "Doc's got me looking much worse than I feel, and certainly much worse than I am."

"Not really, Cap'n. Burns can get infected real easy, especially down here in the tropics. Those burns of yours should be treated properly, not with the stop-gap measures we've been forced to use. You should definitely have stitches on your head, or you're going to a have a scar like this." Elijah pointed to his cheek, then slapped the rail. "You need better care than what we can give you."

"I know I must look like a battle-worn sheik with all this gauze wrapped around my head . . . and as for the scar, long after this war is over I'll wear it proudly." He gripped the clenched black fist that rested on the rail. "Really, Elijah, I'm OK . . . really I am."

"Look, Cap'n, you could go with the LST, get the medical treatment you need, and we could pick you up at Lingayen. The Mate can get us there without your help. I'd feel better if you had a real doctor look at that cut on your head, and redress those burns."

"Elijah, I know you mean well, but no way am I leaving my ship. That's final. Is that clear?" He waited for the message to sink in. The slump in the medic's shoulders told him it had. "Now, I want you to go help Doc get the men who are seriously injured transferred over to the LST."

Elijah shook his head slowly. "You're making a mistake, Cap'n, but I understand." He turned and trudged away, heading for the main deck.

Captain Daly, now joined by Lieutenant Wagner, continued to monitor the process. Just as the last man reached the LST and was lifted to safety, three Navy Corsairs, with their distinctive gull-wing design, screamed over the ships at an altitude of about 300 yards.

"Wow!" huffed Wagner as the air whooshed out of his lungs. "Thank God, those weren't Japs." He looked wide-eyed at the Captain. "All my men, as well as myself, were so interested watching the guys getting shifted to the LST, I doubt any of them saw the planes coming . . . at least not until they were about ten seconds away." He frowned, his eyes narrowing. "The LSTs were probably alerted by the Navy . . . or maybe they saw them on their radar . . . but I wish to hell they'd told us. I damn near pissed in my pants."

The Captain chuckled. "I don't think there's a man on board the *Albert A.* that didn't jump when those babies passed over us." He grinned as he patted Wagner's shoulder. "You've got to admit, they sure are a comforting sight." The three planes shot upward and made a large circle around the ships.

Lieutenant Wagner watched the planes, nodding his head. "I'm sure those Corsairs arriving at this precise time is no coincidence. It's my bet they were sent to coincide with the arrival of the LSTs; to provide cover during the attempt to pull us off the rocks. Had we not broken loose on our own, their timing would have been perfect."

Captain Daly squinted his eyes in thought. "You know, you're right. The three ships, all stationary and together, would have made an easier target for that Jap Betty." He pressed his lips together. "That goes for the mortar teams on shore, too."

Cash had overheard the conversation from his spot on the bridge and stepped out onto the wing. "Wouldn't you know, the Navy sends air support to protect two Navy LSTs, but where were they when the Merchant Marine needed them?"

Wagner, a proud Navy man, glared.

The Mate and the Captain couldn't help the chuckles that escaped from each of them.

Lieutenant Wagner, realizing they'd been pulling his leg, decided to give them a little of their own medicine. With a serious look, he said, "They were probably too busy helping out some other poor lost Merchant Marine ship that had gone one hundred degrees off course and gotten itself grounded on some other Jap-held island." He grinned.

All three men burst out laughing. They entered the bridge together, their laughter subsiding to smiles.

The ships bells struck twice. Captain Daly looked at his watch. "Five o'clock. I know this voyage isn't over yet, and there probably will be more confrontations with the Japs at Lingayen Gulf, but if I live to be a hundred I'll never forget these last thirteen desperate hours."

Epilogue

FOUR HOURS prior to the *Albert A. Robinson* entering Lingayen gulf, two Japanese Kamikaze planes had hedge-hopped over the hills into the harbor. Instead of choosing as their target one of the seven lighter-armed Liberty ships at anchor, they chose to attack a Navy cruiser. But the Zeroes didn't get within a mile of the Navy ship. Apparently, it had been forewarned of the approaching suicide mission.

Two Divine Winds failed to honor their Emperor that day — two less for the crew of the *Albert A.* to worry about in the days to come.

Afterword

IN THE FIRST two years of World War II, 1942 through 1943, casualties aboard Merchant ships (not including the Navy Armed Guard) were greater proportionately than those of all other branches of our Armed Forces combined, with the exception of the U.S. Marine Corps.

Yet little was heard of these Navy men and the civilians of the Merchant Marine who volunteered for this hazardous wartime duty — perhaps due to the "gentlemen's agreement" put into effect immediately after Pearl Harbor between the government and the news media to censor the news of the sinking of all ships for reasons of security. And so, with almost no mention of the heavy losses experienced by the merchant ships in newspapers or on the radio, limited

thought or credit was given to the service of the Merchant Marine, and their part in winning the war was forgotten.

And there was another reason for the news blackout concerning the high number of ships being torpedoed and sunk. In January of 1942, only 55,000 Merchant Marine officers and men were sailing our small but growing fleet of cargo vessels. Fully loaded ships were detained from sailing, due to the lack of qualified crews, at the rate of 40 per month. It was no wonder that the War Shipping Administration (WSA) demanded the censoring of the news. They could ill-afford to have those presently manning the ships, or the experienced sailors with safe, well-paying shore jobs, scared away from signing on to the war effort by the news of so many ships being sunk.

Fortunately, our government had foreseen and prepared for the inevitable war. Shipyards were turning out tankers and Liberty ships in ever-increasing quantities — only compounding the need for more experienced and licensed personnel.

The WSA was forced to form a new government office called Recruitment and Manning Organization (RMO), which set about to recruit the former sailors and officers of the Merchant Marine. Much to the RMO's credit, and the patriotic climate that prevailed all over the USA, over 85,000 experienced sailors who had retired or had been working in shore jobs stepped forward and were signed-on by mid-1943. Many of these men were in their 40s, 50s, and 60s. They were patriots in every sense of the word.

The blackout of information relating to the sinking of Merchant ships continued throughout the war. *Very little knowledge of the war action the Merchant Marine crews and their Navy Armed Guard endured was ever released to the public.*

However, the highest-ranking officers in our other military services, who were in the know, gave testimony to the bravery of those who sailed aboard the Merchant ships.

General Douglas MacArthur, at the conclusion of the Philippine campaign stated,

> With us, they have shared the heaviest enemy fire. I hold no

> branch in higher esteem than the Merchant Marine service.

Fleet Admiral Ernest J. King, Commander in Chief of the United States Navy, noted:

> During the past three and a half years, the Navy has been dependent upon the Merchant Marine to supply our far-flung fleet and bases. Consequently, it is fitting that the Merchant Marine share in our success as it shared in our trials.

And from General Eisenhower, the poignant words of praise:

> Every man in the Allied Command is quick to express his admiration for the loyalty, courage, and fortitude of the officers and men of the Merchant Marine. When final victory is ours, there is no organization that will share its credit more deservedly than the Merchant Marine.

The facts in this Afterword were taken from a report by Vice Admiral Emery Scott Land, USN (Ret), Administrator of the War Shipping Administration (USA) and Chairman of the U.S. Maritime Commission. The report went to President Harry S. Truman on January 15, 1946, as a WSA summary of the U.S. Merchant Marine under his command during World War II. This report can be found at the Office of External Affairs of the U.S. Maritime Administration.

Author's Note

FOR A LIVE introduction to a World War II U.S. Merchant Marine ship, the reader may visit the National Liberty Ship Memorial, the SS *Jeremiah O'Brien*, docked in San Francisco, California, or the SS *John W. Brown*, docked in Baltimore, Maryland. Both ships are open to the public daily.

On your tour, put yourself in the place of the men you have just read about as you walk the bridge, visit its adjoining chart room, and stroll through the cargo holds where tens of thousands of U.S. troops were quartered. Below you can see the mammoth 140-ton, 2,500 horse-power triple expansion steam engine and its 16-foot rocker arms. (If you saw the movie *Titanic*, when the drama in the engine was filmed, you were actually seeing the engine room of the *Jeremiah O'Brien*.)

Up forward or back aft you will see the 20mm antiaircraft guns, and can sit in the saddle of the U.S. Navy Armed Guard's 3 inch/50 cannons.

. . . And don't forget Sparks's radio shack. Perhaps I'll be there.

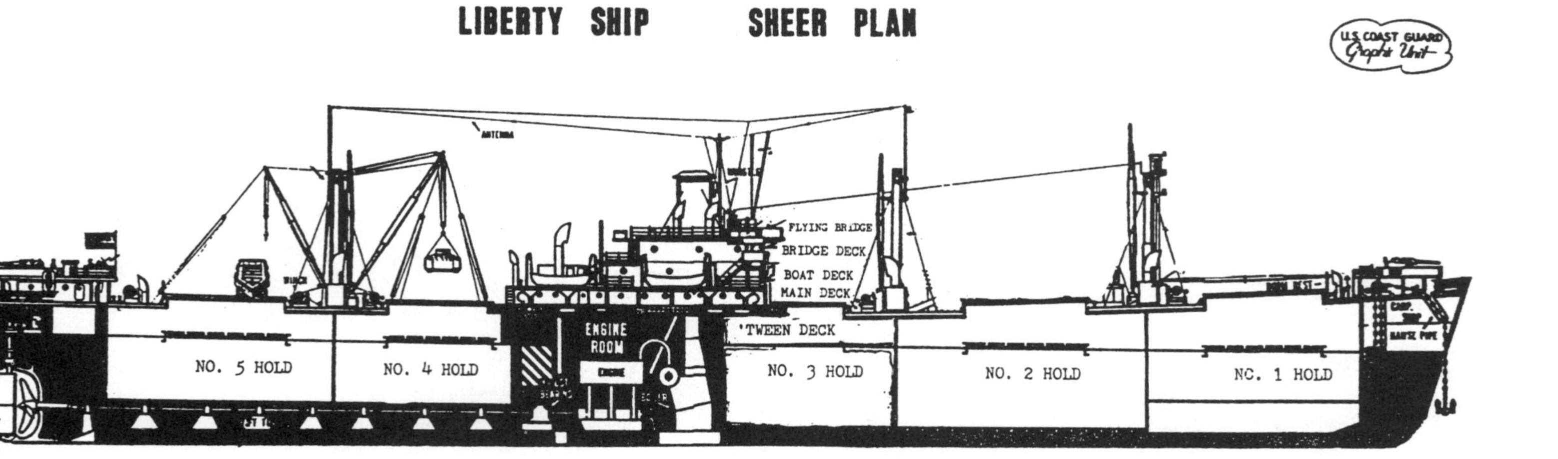

Liberty Ship Upper Decks

LIBERTY SHIP UPPER DECKS

Boat Deck

A. & B. Port side life boats
C. & D. Starboard side life boats
E., L., M., N. Engineer's quarters
G., H., I. Deck officer's quarters
J. Two ass't radio operator's
K. Small hospital beds
O. Purser & medic quarters
P. Fiddley (smoke hole & vent)
Q. Port outside deck
R. Starboard outside deck
S. Boat deck companionway

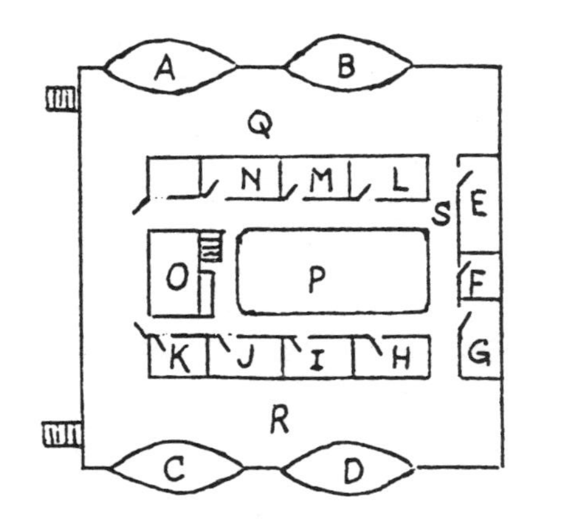

Bridge Deck

A. Port side bridge wing
B. Starboard side bridge wing
C. The ship's bridge & wheel-house
D. Bridge rear deck
E. Potato bin
F. Chief Radio Operator's quarters
G. Gunnery officer's quarters
H. Radio (shack) room
I. Chart room
J. Captain's quarters
K. Fiddley (smoke hole & vent)
L. Bridge deck companionway

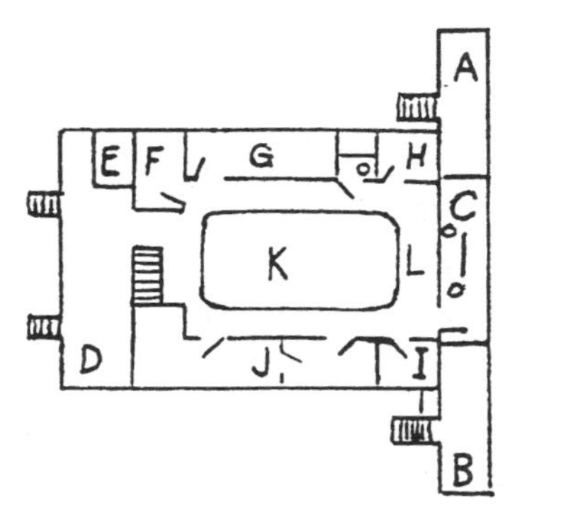

Flying Bridge

A. Port side signal light
B. Starboard side signal light
C. & D. Ladders down to bridge deck
E. Smoke stack
F. Flying bridge wheel & compass
5 & 7 Port side 20 mm gun tubs
4 & 6 Starboard side 20 mm gun tubs

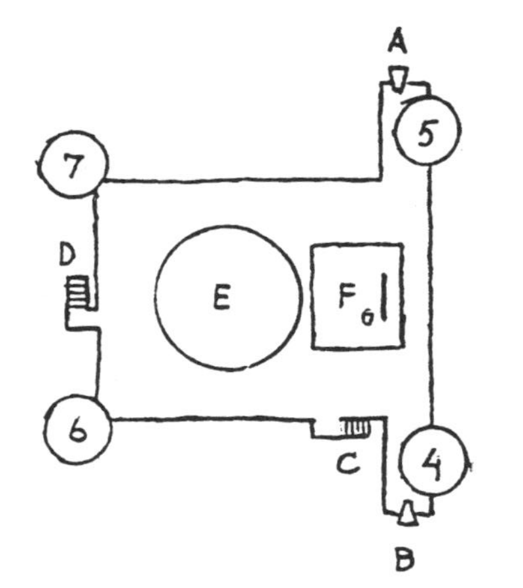

Thirteen Desperate Hours was co-authored by Will and Marilyn Rayment, who write under the pen-name "Marill Johnson." Will, as the storyteller, was actually Chief Radio Officer ("Sparks") aboard the *Albert A. Robinson.*

Will quit high school in 1943 at age 16, as did many of the boys in the sophomore class. They were going to "win the war." Will studied a "crash radio operator's course" and passed his FCC Radio Telegraph technical and code exam in late 1943. With license in hand, he joined the Merchant Marine, which was in desperate need of licensed radio operators — so desperate that his first ship had to borrow two unlicensed Navy men to fill the watches.

On the day Will picked up his Seaman's ID and Coast Guard pass, he was sent to the Richmond, California, Refinery to board his first ship, the T-2 tanker, *Mission Santa Cruz.* And then it was off to the South Pacific theater of war. At the age of 17, with an Ensign's rating as Chief Radio Officer, he was among the youngest officers in the Merchant Marine.

Will served 36 months of sea duty on five different ships: *Mission Santa Cruz* (T-2 tanker), *Gilbert M. Hitchcock* (a Liberty Ship), *Albert A. Robinson*, *Grommet Reefer* (a refrigeration ship), and the *Fenn Victory* (a Victory ship). During his 36 months of sea duty he experienced the transporting of munitions, volatile petroleum, and troops, as well as air bombings, typhoons, and even a tsunami (tidal wave).

In 1948, at age 22, he married Marilyn, his co-author, and they have enjoyed the good life he fought for more than 50 years ago.